KT-227-704

THE GIRL OUTSIDE

Holly Tolliver's head — and heart — were awhirl. As the penniless protegée of wealthy old Mrs. Lamont, she'd led such a quiet life that she'd never had a date. Now Mrs. Lamont was dead and Holly's future was in the hands of the three sophisticated young heirs. Overnight she was plunged into the glamorous Palm Beach society life, pursued by both a fascinating millionaire and a handsome playboy.

GEORGIA CRAIG

THE GIRL OUTSIDE

Complete and Unabridged

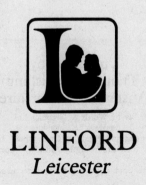

LINFORD
Leicester

First published in the
United States of America

First Linford Edition
published 1997

Copyright © 1960 by Arcadia House
All rights reserved

British Library CIP Data

Craig, Georgia
   The girl outside.—Large print ed.—
Linford romance library
1. Love stories
2. Large type books
I. Title
823.9′14 [F]

ISBN 0–7089–5113–9

Published by
F. A. Thorpe (Publishing) Ltd.
Anstey, Leicestershire

Set by Words & Graphics Ltd.
Anstey, Leicestershire
Printed and bound in Great Britain by
T. J. International Ltd., Padstow, Cornwall

This book is printed on acid-free paper

1

HOLLY sat perfectly still on the huge stump, her jeans-clad legs drawn up beneath her, and watched the huge rattlesnake slither past the stump and lose itself in the jungle-like under-growth beside the path. It must have been a snake like that, she told herself as she watched the hideous length disappear, that had killed her father when she was two.

She was very much at home in these woods that separated Hacienda del Sol from the acres of lush citrus groves that had for many years supported the Lamont family. But from earliest childhood she had been taught that she shared these woods with huge rattlesnakes, and must be very careful when she walked there.

Right now, she told herself as the snake disappeared, she had a lot more on her mind than the reptiles that were so plentiful in this area. Back at Hacienda del Sol, her fate was being decided by three strangers who were Granny Lamont's family: her great-grandchildren who had paid the stern old woman so little attention all their lives but who, the moment she died, had gathered at Hacienda del Sol to settle her estate, and who were obviously a trifle puzzled and resentful at being faced with the problem of settling Holly's future as well.

Holly could understand their feelings. After all, she had no claim on the family; she was not a Lamont. She was only the daughter of the man who had been Granny's trusted overseer and good friend. The Tollivers had been overseers at Hacienda del Sol as long as the Lamonts had been owners. They had come there together many years ago, that first Tolliver and that first Lamont. The two young men had been close friends, and the mere fact that Lamont had money to buy

2

and develop the groves that became famous, and that Tolliver had had nothing but strength and youth and a devotion to his friend, hadn't seemed to either of the two men important. They had worked together, the hard, grueling work of clearing the jungle in inland Florida, where the soil had been so perfect for growing citrus; and as the groves had increased, and with them, their employees, theirs had been a common cause.

When Walker Lamont brought his bride there, sixty-five years ago, there had been an Eben Tolliver and his young wife waiting to greet them. And the two women had been friends, against the all but unbearable loneliness of the jungle.

When Eben Tolliver's son grew up and married, there was work for him, of course. He had been sent away to the University, at Lamont expense, to be taught the latest methods of growing and marketing citrus fruit, and had married and brought his wife back.

And the cycle had gone on, Lamonts and Tollivers, so there were times when it was hard to remember which was the employer, which the employee.

Granny had outlived the others. But now Granny, too, was dead, at ninety-one. A rich, full life she had boasted, and she would not have had one year of it changed. There had been children; they had gone off to school and had not come back. They had married and raised families, and once in a great while one or the other of them visited the Hacienda for a few days. But its isolation, its lack of any entertaining facilities soon depressed them.

Holly's father, still as devoted to the Lamonts as his own father had been, had died of a rattlesnake bite when Holly was two; and Granny, as Holly had been taught to call her from the first, had taken Holly and her mother to live with her at the Hacienda. Granny had been lonely, and she had loved the child and her mother. They had lived quietly but contentedly. Holly had been sent to the school in the nearest village, six miles away, where she made friends, of course. But she was happiest at the Hacienda. At sixteen she had lost her mother, but she and Granny had still clung together. Granny had said, "Now we're the family, Holly — you and I. The others — my own grandchildren — I wouldn't know them if I met them on the street. But you and I, Holly — *we're* a family."

Remembering all this, Holly wept silently from the bitter grief and loneliness of Granny's death. The gentle, kind old woman had died quietly in her sleep. Holly had tried to accept the comforting assurance of the clergyman who conducted the funeral, and the doctor who had known and admired the old woman for many years, that it was a painless, easy death, that Granny had lived out her full span and that she had been very tired, and no doubt quite willing to go.

But Holly hadn't been willing. Holly

had been, and still was, heartbroken. The arrival of Granny's three grandchildren, heirs to the estate, had been inevitable, of course. But they were so frightening! To a girl brought up as Holly had been, there was something downright terrifying about their sleekness, their complete almost arrogant self-assurance; the way in which they had calmly taken over the whole place, ignoring her, as though she did not exist. And, of course, she wasn't one of the family. Granny had never adopted her; it had never seemed to either of them necessary.

She had slipped out of the house when the three of them settled down in the big, shabby old library to discuss what was to be done about the place. She dared not think what they might be planning for *her* future, or even if they felt there was any need to plan for her!

As a matter of fact, the question of her future was at the moment receiving considerable attention from the three grandchildren.

Caro Beardsley, the eldest of the three, a slim, elegant if by no means beautiful woman of thirty-two, was saying crisply to her two brothers, "It's perfectly absurd even to consider the girl. Thank heaven Gran never legally adopted her, so I can't see why we should feel any responsibility for her at all. Gran didn't even mention her in her will."

"Which was made years ago, shortly after her husband's death, and probably forgotten," Walker Lamont reminded his sister. "I suppose Gran, if she ever thought of the matter at all, was quite sure she could trust us to do the decent thing for the girl."

Charles Lamont, the youngest of the three, lounged in a deep chair, one leg thrown over the arm, his dark eyes traveling from his sister to his brother. There was a faint quirk of amusement about his thin, handsome mouth.

"Question is," he drawled amiably, "what *is* the decent thing for the girl? After all, this is the only home she's ever known. She was brought up here in this wild jungle. Where would she go? What would she do if we turn her out?

Caro bristled indignantly, her eyes cold.

"I really can't see that's our problem," she said stiffly. "After all, she's been cared for by Gran since she was two; fed, housed, clothed, educated. Now she's eighteen years old. High time, I think, that she should be thinking for herself, not depending on us to provide for her."

Walker Lamont eyed his sister curiously, as though he didn't like her too well.

"She's little more than a child, Caro," he pointed out. "Living here, taking care of Gran, when none of us in the family ever came near the old girl — it seems to me that entitles the girl to something."

"Well, after all, if Gran had wanted to provide for her, she could have said so in her will," Caro protested.

8

"If we could just let her stay on here with these two antediluvian servants — " Charles began.

"Oh, Chuck, don't be a fool!" Caro said sharply. "You know we've got a fabulous offer for the place and we're going to sell! We'll never get another such offer. It's a perfect spot for a swank hunting and fishing club, and we'd be fools not to grab it, especially since the groves have already been sold. Remember, about all Gran left was the real estate — there was barely enough cash to pay off current obligations and funeral expenses."

Walker said sharply, "Look, let's come to some decision. We've got a hundred miles to drive back to Palm Beach, I have plane reservations for a 10:45 plane, I've got to be in New York tomorrow. Now, what are we going to do with the girl?"

Charles said gently, "Why don't you take her home with you, Caro?"

"What?" Caro was startled, outraged, incredulous that he could be serious.

9

"Why, yes, that's an excellent suggestion, Chuck. I'm surprised that you thought of it," Walker said quickly.

"Oh, now and then I have brief periods of brilliance," Charles answered modestly, his dark eyes brimming with cynical amusement as he watched Caro's convulsed face.

"Well, I don't think it's an excellent suggestion and I'll have no part of it," Caro sputtered furiously. "I will not be saddled with the girl. I just won't!"

"She won't take up much room," said Charles gently, needing her deftly and deliberately. "And maybe she can help take care of the children."

Caro all but choked at the idea.

"Help take care of the children?" she repeated furiously. "Why, Miss Endicott would give notice immediately if *I* so much as suggested that I'd like to help with the children. I have to ask her permission even to *see* them!"

Charles asked curiously, "Who's Miss Endicott?"

"My perfect jewel of an English

nanny," Caro answered. "She's a treasure, and half of my friends with children are simply dying to get her away from me. I'm certainly not going to risk losing her just to have that big-eyed, gawky, stupid-looking girl in my house!"

"Hi, now, wait a minute!" Walker protested. "She's a very lovely girl — and I'm sure she's not stupid. She's probably afraid of you."

"Which would make having her in my house pure joy for both of us, wouldn't it?" Caro asked, thin-lipped, anger aflame in her dark eyes.

"I've an idea," said Charles amiably. When the other two looked at him suspiciously, he gave them a boyish grin and said, "Why don't we find her a nice rich husband?"

"Oh, don't be a fool, Chuck," Caro snapped.

"Well, properly dressed, smartened up a bit, she'd be a very lovely girl and ought to be quite appealing to some of the fellows we all know," Charles insisted. When he and his sister came into the same room arguments always developed, and with Charles it was a matter of pride always to take the opposite view, regardless of which side of the argument his sister was on.

"I'm afraid there's no other way out, Caro, for the present," Walker said firmly. "It will be only temporary, of course."

"Just until we find her a husband," Charles contributed gently.

"I will not sponsor that girl socially," snapped Caro hotly. "I won't drag her around, present her to my friends. I suppose, if she has to, she can come and stay at the villa, but it's got to be only temporary, just for the season. By that time, you'll have to make some other arrangements for her, Walker. I simply will *not* be burdened with her for more than a few weeks."

Charles was watching her curiously, and for a moment there was compassion in his eyes for the girl they were

discussing; compassion for Holly and a deep-rooted dislike for his sister.

"What a gay, gladsome time the kid's going to have, for sure," he mocked gently. "Cinderella had it good compared to what's going to happen to this chick."

"Then it's settled," said Walker, and heaved a sigh of relief and consulted his watch. "I suppose we may as well take her back with us. No point in having to make another trip out here, now that all the details of the sale of the property are being attended to by our attorneys."

He walked, without waiting for an answer, to the old-fashioned bellrope and pulled it hard.

A moment later a tiny old woman, stooped and wrinkled, appeared in the doorway and looked from one to the other speechlessly. Walker said curtly, "Send Miss Holly here, please. And you'd better pack her things. We're taking her back to Palm Beach with us."

The wrinkled old face was touched with a shy smile.

"Oh, I'm that glad, Mr. Lamont, sir," she said eagerly. "I didn't want to think of the child here alone now that the old lady is gone."

Caro flung the woman an irritated glance.

"Haven't you heard that the place is being sold?" she snapped.

The old woman eyed her curiously, and the eager smile was gone.

"Oh, yes, ma'am. Mrs. Lamont said that was what would happen as soon as she closed her eyes in her final sleep," she said quietly. "That's why she gave me and Sam our house and set up a trust fund for us ten years ago."

She turned and hobbled away, and Caro said furiously, "If that's the sort of thing that's been going on here, no wonder there was so little money left in the estate!"

"Beardsley hasn't lost his wad, has he?" asked Charles gently.

"Don't be vulgar!" snapped Caro.

14

"I was just wondering why you're so all-fired anxious to get your hands on some cash, when Beardsley is so rich it's indecent," Charles pointed out reasonably.

"I wish," Walker sighed, "just once you two could be in the same room without fireworks."

"What a wish, pal. What a wish!" Charles murmured.

"One that's not likely to be fulfilled, I'm afraid," Walker admitted wryly. "I wonder where the dickens the girl is."

A moment later Holly came into the big hall. Caro called to her sharply, "We've been waiting for you. Come here."

Charles looked at her swiftly, frowning. It was a tone she would not have dared use to one of the servants in her Palm Beach villa, knowing the servant would instantly have walked out. And once again Charles felt a deep compassion for this girl, and the future that would be hers in Caro's home.

He studied the girl as Walker

explained what they had planned. She was not much more than five feet tall, and her body, even in the faded jeans and thin shirt, was graceful. Her hair, the blackest Charles had ever seen, was thick and curled about her oval face, sun-tanned and lit with enormous incredibly blue eyes. The girl *was* a beauty, he told himself, as he saw her expressive face touched with dismay and shock at the news that she was going to stay with Caro for a while. Obviously, Charles told himself, the poor kid was terrified at the idea. He glanced at his sister, and decided he didn't blame the girl. Caro could really be an ugly customer when things didn't go to suit her.

"It's very kind of Mrs. Beardsley," Holly said when Walker had announced their impending departure. "But I'd much rather just stay on here. It's my home."

"Well, it won't be in a few more days," Caro cut in curtly. "We're selling the place."

Holly turned to stare at Caro, and the blood seeped away from her face until it looked drawn.

"Oh, *no!*" she whispered as at a prospect too horrible to contemplate. "Oh, you can't do that. Why, the latest planting won't be bearing until next year, and Granny had just made a wonderful deal for the year's crop to a fruit-juice processing plant."

"The groves have been sold, too, Holly; they will be kept up, and the contracts Grandmother Lamont made will be honored," Walker said. "The house and twenty acres of uncleared land have been sold to a group who are going to turn it into a hunting and fishing club."

"So don't be difficult, Holly," Caro cut in sharply. "Run along and get dressed. That old witch of a servant woman is packing for you. We're leaving as soon as you're ready."

Holly stared at her, blue eyes wide and dark with shock.

"But, Mrs. Beardsley, I can't pack all

of my things in just a few minutes. I've lived here all my life," she told her.

Caro's face hardened slightly.

"An inventory will be taken before the papers are signed on the sale, and anything here that is yours will be packed and placed in storage for you until you have time to make plans for your future," she said icily. "All you need take with you now are actual necessities, such as your clothes — if you have any."

Her eyes raked the blue jeans and shirt, the scuffed loafers on the girl's feet with a contemptuous gleam.

Charles studied his sister curiously, and then looked at the girl expectantly. But as the girl's shoulders drooped and she turned away like a frightened but docile child, the expectant look faded from his eyes. He listened for a moment to the soft sound of the girl's footsteps on the stairs, and then he reached for a cigarette.

"Hasn't much spirit, has she?" he commented dryly.

Walker looked sharply at him.

"None of us ever knew Grandmother Lamont at all well." he stated flatly, "but from all I've heard of the old girl, living with her under complete domination for sixteen years would be enough to steamroller the spirit out of 'most anybody."

"It's good that she is so spiritless," said Caro grimly. "It will make it much easier for me having her around. But mind you, Walker, you've got to make other arrangements before the season is over."

2

BY the time Holly came down, wearing the neat, inexpensive navy blue dress with its soft white collar and carrying an ancient suitcase, the argument in the big dim room had reached an acrimonious stage.

Caro took one look at the girl in the doorway, groaned and covered her eyes with her hand as though the sight were more than she could endure.

Walker asked, "We thought perhaps you might like to go away to school, Holly."

"I've been to school, Mr. Lamont," Holly answered, steadying her voice with an effort. "I graduated from high school in June."

"Oh, well, then, school would be out of the question." Walker smiled at her pleasantly, but her fear of these strangers who had suddenly descended on her was too great to permit her to smile back.

Caro stood up, gathered her sable scarf, her bag and gloves, and said crisply, "Then if you're ready — Holly, surely you have better luggage than that? A decent dress?"

Color burned hotly in Holly's cheeks and her eyes were ashamed.

"I've never had any use for luggage," she explained shakily. "I've never been anywhere. And this is my best dress. I never dressd up much here, and I've outgrown my school clothes. And here I've worn — well, play-suits and shorts and jeans."

"Looks as though she's going to give you a swell chance to indulge in your favorite sport, Caro darling," drawled Charles, and smiled at Holly as he picked up the suitcase. "Shall we get moving? I've got a heavy date in Palm Beach tonight."

"And I'm giving a dinner party," wailed Caro as she glanced at Holly and shuddered visibly.

Outside in the mid-afternoon sunshine of a November day, the car stood waiting, a long, sleek, expensive-looking car. As Charles stowed Holly's bag in the back, he smiled at her and said quietly, "You'd better ride up front with me, Holly. Be more comfortable for you."

Holly's voice shook as she thanked him faintly, and because she was blinded by tears she stumbled as she sought to step into the car. Charles put out his hand swiftly and steadied her.

Walker and Caro got into the back, and Caro said sharply, "Now, mind you, Chuck, none of your wild driving! I have a family that's counting on me."

"For what, I often wonder?" Charles answered as he slid beneath the wheel. "Miss Endicott looks after the babies, Hubert has his 'gentleman's gentleman' who does everything for him but breathe, and you have a housekeeper who bosses the servants. I can't see that you're the indispensable woman, Caro darling — but I have plans for myself, so don't worry. I'll drive circumspectly, I assure you."

The car slid forward so that whatever answer Caro might have made was lost in the sudden movement.

The car swooped past the airport and along the boulevard to a cream-colored bridge that spanned the waters of Lake Worth where small charter fishing boats were chugging home after the day's sport. Finally it swung through a wide gate and came to a halt at steps leading into a large, imposing house. Holly had a confused impression of luxuriantly flowering shrubbery and velvety lawns. Beyond where they had stopped was the glimmer of a swimming pool, so close to the Atlantic Ocean.

A white-coated houseman appeared as if by magic and accepted Holly's battered suitcase with a wooden lack of expression that was, in itself, an expression of shocked incredulity.

"Sorry I can't invite you to dinner, Chuck," Caro began.

"Thanks a whole heck of a lot, Caro, but I've got a dinner date."

"And I'd ask you, Walker, except that it's a formal party and I don't see how I could possibly add another place," Caro went on as she got out of the car and turned to Holly, her eyes chilling. "Well, come on."

As the girl got out of the car, Chuck's eyes followed her, and he leaned toward Caro.

"You will see that she's fed, won't you, Caro, even if you can't include her in your party?" he drawled. Before Caro could master her anger sufficiently to answer, he added, to Holly, smiling, "Goodbye and good luck, kid — you'll probably need it."

Holly lifted her eyes to his for just a moment and tried to smile. But it was little more than a tight-lipped grimace, and the misery in her eyes made them seem almost black.

"Goodbye," said Walker briskly, and avoided the girl's eyes. "I'll be in touch with you, Caro."

24

"You'd better be," Caro answered, and there was an ominous note in her voice. She turned toward the house, over her shoulder ordering Holly to follow her, with the white-coated houseman bringing up the rear. He carried the ancient suitcase gingerly as though he expected it to disintegrate in his hands.

Inside the house Caro turned to the houseman.

"Where is Mrs. Weston, Luther? Send her here, please."

"Immediately, Madam," said Luther, putting down the suitcase as though highly relieved to be rid of it and disappearing down the hall and through a swinging door.

Caro waited, not even looking at Holly. A moment later, a middle-aged woman, severely dressed in black, her graying hair pulled into a tight bun at the back of her head, appeared, and Caro turned to her with frank relief.

"Mrs. Weston, this is Holly Tolliver. She'll be staying here for a few days.

I'm sure you can find a place to put her. Look after it, will you?" Caro gave the order curtly and, without waiting for an answer, went swiftly up the stairs.

Holly tried hard not to shrink from the cold, measuring look in Mrs. Weston's dark eyes, hoping against hope that there would be a gleam of kindness there and knowing somehow there would not be.

"So you're staying a few days," Mrs. Weston commented dryly. "I'll send someone to show you to a room."

Once more she vanished down the hall, and Holly leaned against the stair railing, her knees trembling, fighting with every ounce of courage and strength she possessed not to burst into tears.

At last a neatly uniformed maid appeared, gave her a shy smile, and picked up the battered suitcase.

"If you'll come this way, miss?" she suggested, and led the way up the stairs.

Holly stumbled after her, clinging to the stair railing, feeling that she would surely fall if she didn't. At the top of the stairs the maid walked on to a corridor that ran across the house, forming a T above the stairs. At the far end she stopped, opened a door, and stood aside for Holly to enter.

It was a small room and the furnishings were somewhat shabby. Obviously, though Holly could not realize it, the room lay in the servants' wing.

The maid set down the suitcase, eyed Holly appraisingly and asked, "Are you going to be the new maid?"

"I don't know," Holly said faintly.

The maid smiled. "Well, don't you worry. The Madam's sure to find something for you to do. I'll get you some tea."

"Thank you," said Holly, and blinked against the tears. "You're awfully kind!"

The maid's eyebrows went up slightly in obvious surprise.

"Well, for Pete's sake!" she answered vigorously. "I was new here myself a couple of seasons ago. It's scary, and no one knows it better than I do. All the others are trained and smart as anything. Me, I'm just a local gal trying to get enough training to be sure I can keep a job like this. My name's Mary. What's yours?"

"Holly."

"That's cute. Bet you were a Christmas baby!"

Holly's heart warmed slightly.

"Christmas Eve," she answered, and managed a faint smile.

"Look," said Mary, "have you had any dinner?"

"No, and I didn't have any lunch. I couldn't eat. Someone I loved very much has just died." Her voice broke.

"Gee, I'm sorry," said Mary gently. "Well, you wait right here and I'll see what I can sneak past the chef. He's one of those guys who has a nice, even disposition — he's always mad! But I'll get you something."

"Don't go to any trouble."

Mary stared at her.

"Boy, I'll bet that's the first time anybody ever said that in this house," she admitted. "Most of the people here don't give a darn how much trouble they cause. They seem to feel that the more trouble they can cause the more important they are!"

She flashed Holly a friendly grin and disappeared through the door.

Holly felt warmed and comforted by the girl's unself-conscious friendliness and set about the small task of unpacking her few belongings. Memories of life at Hacienda del Sol threatened her with tears, but she fought them down as best she could. When a little later Mary came back bearing a daintily appointed tray, Holly was sitting at the window, looking out into the darkness, listening to the unaccustomed sound of the sea splashing against the beach.

Mary put down the tray, and Holly was startled to see the anger on Mary's face.

"I hope it will be quite satisfactory, miss," she said stiffly. "Mrs. Weston arranged it herself."

"I'm sure it will be, Mary, and thanks."

Mary flashed hotly, "You might have told me you were a guest, instead of letting me make a fool of myself."

Puzzled, Holly asked, "What do you mean?"

"You know darned well what I mean," snapped Mary. "And if you want to, run to Madam and get me fired, you snoop!"

Holly stared at her, bewildered.

"Honestly, Mary — " she began.

"Letting me think you were a new maid. And why wouldn't I, seeing you stuck here in the servants' wing?" snapped Mary hotly. "And Mrs. Weston saying you were a house guest. If you are, what are you doing here, unless Madam's brought you in to spy on us and to tattle-tale to her if we don't do our work right. Well, go ahead and tell her — I don't care!

There are other jobs. I wanted a good reference from her, because that would make it easy to get a good job."

"Mary, I don't know *what* I am here," Holly cut in. "I'd like to be a new maid here and I'm quite sure I'm not a house guest. I'm just here until they decide what to do with me. I lived with old Mrs. Lamont until she died two weeks ago, and Mrs. Beardsley and her brothers sold the place. I guess they didn't know what to do with me, so *she* said I could come here for a little while."

Mary stared at her, wide-eyed.

"Is that on the level?" she demanded.

"Of course, Mary. I wouldn't lie to you. You're the first person who has shown me any friendliness. I'm very grateful, Mary!"

"Well, I'll be darned," said Mary. "That's one for the book!"

But she had relaxed a little, and once more her smile was warm.

"Well, when Mrs. Weston said I was to serve your meals to you here even if you did have a room in the servants' wing, I took it for granted you'd been sent to spy on us." She grinned and added, "That's the way I get most of my exercise — jumping to conclusions!"

Mary grinned, nodded and went out. And Holly, warmed and comforted by the girl's unaffected friendliness, found that she was hungry and settled down gratefully to the delicious meal on the tray before her.

3

IN the morning when Mary came to bring her breakfast, Holly greeted her warmly, and Mary responded cheerfully.

"You must have slept well," said Mary, placing the covered dishes on the small table where Holly had had her dinner last night. "You look swell. Look, when you've finished your breakfast, why don't you go down on the beach for a while? It's a super-duper morning, but of course you couldn't swim. It's a bit too chilly for that before noon."

"I can't swim anyway," Holly answered. "For one thing, I don't have a suit. We didn't have a swimming pool at the Hacienda, and I've never seen the ocean. We used to go to Ft. Myers now and then to shop — oh, maybe two or three times a year — but that's the Gulf. And there was never any occasion to learn to swim."

Mary studied her curiously, and then she lifted her shoulders in a little shrug.

"Well, go take a walk and have a look at the ocean. It's quite a sight this morning," she said briskly. "No use staying all shut up here all day. Come on, I'll show you a short cut. You won't want to use the front stairs. Too much traffic there this morning."

Holly followed her to the end of the corridor, to a door that opened out on a narrow balcony where stairs led down to the side and from there to the beach.

Holly thanked her and went back to her breakfast. Afterwards she put her room to rights and then walked down the corridor, along the balcony and down the steps that led to the path that in turn led to the beach. There were high, wide steps leading over the bulkhead that was supposed to hold back the ocean in stormy weather. Holly paused at the top of the steps, breathless before her first view of the ocean. She'd been born and had lived all her life in Florida, but so far inland that she had never seen the ocean before.

The water was blue, many shades deeper in color than the arching sky, and the great rolling breakers were laced with white foam as they splashed against the yellow sand and slid back again. She walked down the beach steps and along the beach, watching the sand-pipers busy with each receding wave, listening to the strange, unmusical cry of the gulls as they flew overhead. A flight of pelicans floated by; then the leader lifted and dropped his wings, and all along the line of eight or ten there was a rippling movement as each gull imitated in turn the leader's gesture.

"Interesting beggars, aren't they?" said a friendly voice behind her. She turned, startled, to face a middle-aged man, not very much taller than she, with a lean, sun-browned body clad only in brief blue bathing trunks. The wiriness of his body seemed much more youthful than his lined face beneath a thatch of silver-white hair. His eyes were blue and gentle, and his smile was warm.

"Oh, you mean the pelicans? They *are* funny, aren't they?" Holly agreed, delighted to find someone besides Mary who could be friendly.

"I've always been intrigued by the way they fly in formation," said the man. "If there are only two, one is the leader and the other flies behind him, imitating everything he does."

He studied her curiously, but the look in his eyes robbed the curiosity of anything even faintly offensive.

"I'm afraid I don't know you, do I?" he asked.

"No, I'm Holly Tolliver, and I only arrived last night," Holly answered. "Do you work here?"

"Why, yes, as a matter of fact, I do."

There was the faintest possible twinkle in his blue eyes, but his tone was quite grave. "Do you?"

Holly shook her head and explained her presence. As she gave the story briefly, succinctly, the man's expression altered slightly. But before he could say anything, a white-coated man bearing a tray came down the beach steps and moved toward the *cabaña*.

"Have you had breakfast?" the stranger asked Holly.

"Oh, yes, thank you. Mary brought it to my room."

"In the servants' wing, I think you said?"

"Why, yes."

The man's hand cupped her elbow and turned her in the direction of the cabaña, saying firmly, "Well, you must come and have some more coffee. I loathe eating alone, even at breakfast."

Holly blinked and looked up at him, startled.

"I'm Hubert Beardsley, Holly," the man told her quietly.

"Caro — Mrs. Beardsley's husband?" Holly gasped.

The man winced ever so slightly and smiled ruefully.

"I've seldom heard it more accurately expressed," he admitted. "Yes, I'm Mrs. Beardsley's husband."

Flushed and miserable. Holly stammered, "I'm sorry. I didn't mean — "

"Of course you didn't." Hubert smiled at her, as they reached the cabaña where the white-coated servant was laying the breakfast tray on a small table. "Wilkins, Miss Tolliver is joining me for breakfast. Lay another place, please."

The man bowed and went into the cabaña, a neat white stucco bungalow, and came back with another service.

"I'll just have some coffee, if I may," Holly protested. "That is, if there's enough for two."

Hubert poured from the tall glass pot, kept hot by a candle burning beneath it.

"There's always about twice as much

as I can drink, and besides, Wilkins wouldn't mind getting a re-fill, would you, Wilkins?"

"Certainly not, sir," Wilkins answered politely.

He bowed and went away back up the beach stairs. Hubert began chatting pleasantly with Holly. He seemed to have all the time in the world, and they lingered pleasurably over breakfast. He led her on to talk about Gran and the Hacienda, and Holly did not realize how much of herself and of her inmost thoughts she was revealing to him. But as she chatted with him, his eyes darkened a little and his jaw set hard because she was giving him a picture of the present generation of Lamonts, including his wife, that he did not like at all.

Eventually Wilkins murmured something deferentially to Hubert, who looked up, nodded and rose, smiling at Holly.

"Thanks for making the breakfast hour so pleasant, Holly," he told her. "I hope you will join me again, perhaps early enough for a swim before breakfast. It gives one a fine appetite."

"You're awfully kind," Holly told him gratefully. "I don't swim, though."

Hubert smiled. "We'll have to remedy that. I'm an excellent teacher."

"Thank you. I think I'd like that."

"Good! Then it's a date," said Hubert. He smiled at her and went away across the beach and up the steps to the terrace.

"More coffee, miss?" suggested Wilkins, poising the half-empty pot above her cup.

"Oh, goodness, no, Mr. Wilkins," Holly protested, laughing. "I've had enough for three breakfasts."

Wilkins hesitated, but he had watched and listened unobtrusively while she and Hubert chatted, and now he spoke deferentially.

"If you will permit me a word, miss?"

"Of course, Mr. Wilkins."

40

"One does not address the servants here as 'Mr.' I'm simply Wilkins, miss."

Color poured into Holly's face and her eyes were shamed.

"I'm sorry, Mr. — I mean Wilkins," she apologized. "I'm not accustomed to this sort of thing. At the Hacienda, all of us, the two servants, Gran and I were — well, we were all family."

"I quite understand, miss." Wilkins smiled, and the smile transformed his homely, middle-aged face that had worn so wooden an expression. "I only mentioned it in the hope of sparing you embarrassment in the future."

"I know." Holly managed a smile. "And I'm very grateful."

"It's quite all right, miss," said Wilkins, once more his expressionless self as he began to clear the table.

Holly got up and walked across the beach, loth to return to the house.

4

HUBERT kept his promise to give her swimming lessons, and the morning hours rapidly became the highlight of her day. The cabaña consisted of one hugh room, furnished in gay colors, running heavily to white-iron furniture and brilliantly patterned chintz. There was a small but well equipped kitchenette, and opening on either side, dressing rooms. There was an ample supply of swim suits, and Holly was delighted to find one that was an acceptable fit.

Hubert expressed himself as delighted with the progress she made under his instructions. Holly loved the exercise, the feel of the water against her — so blue that she almost expected to find herself colored by it as she came out. Wrapped in a terry-cloth beachrobe, she joined Hubert on the glass-enclosed terrace for breakfast.

She sighed happily one morning and surveyed the cabaña.

"I'd like to live here," she said contentedly. "It's — oh, like a doll's house. The Hacienda was so big and so old. This is gay and young and pretty! There are even books to read!"

Hubert laughed as he buttered a muffin.

"Now don't tell me you read books, Holly!" he protested.

Wide-eyed, Holly answered, "Doesn't everybody?"

"I'm afraid not many people I know do," Hubert confessed. "Shame, too, when books are really the best friends a person can have."

"That's what Gran always said," Holly told him. "We had some wonderful books: classics, of course. Nothing new or modern. Gran didn't approve of modern fiction."

"Gran sounds more and more like somebody I wish I had had the chance to know."

"I wish you had, too. She'd have liked you."

"Thank you, Holly. From what you've told me of Gran, I'm sure that's a very real compliment."

"She didn't like a great many people. They thought she was harsh and — well, bossy. Some of the workers were terrified of her; not those who'd been on the place long enough to really know her, but the migrant workers were only there seasonally. It took a long time really to get to know her."

Hubert nodded and skillfully led her on to talk of the life she had lived at the Hacienda. When at last Wilkins murmured in his ear and he rose to go, he looked down at Holly kindly.

"Stay here at the cabaña as much as you like, Holly," he told her gently. "And if you run out of books to read, Wilkins will show you the library." He broke off and cocked an eyebrow at Wilkins, a twinkle in his eyes. "There *is* a library, isn't there, Wilkins?"

"Oh, yes, sir," Wilkins answered.

"I'm sure Mrs. Weston would allow Miss Tolliver to use it."

"Well, now, that's big of Mrs. Weston." Hubert's twinkle vanished.

"It's only, sir, that some of the books are very rare and very valuable and there are people who borrow books and don't return them, and Mrs. Weston felt — "

"I quite understand," said Hubert, and the twinkle, much more faint now, was back. "Very knowledgeable woman, Mrs. Weston."

"Oh, yes, sir — very, sir," Wilkins agreed politely.

"Well, if Miss Tolliver wants to visit the library, Wilkins, you will see to it, won't you? Tell Mrs. Weston it's on my orders."

"Very good, sir." Wilkins was once more his well-trained, expressionless self as he began clearing the table.

"Oh, but I'm sure there are more books here at the cabaña than I'll have time to read," Holly protested, a little disturbed by the exchange. "And maybe Mr. Lamont will have some plans for me before I finish reading all of them."

"No doubt," agreed Hubert, almost as expressionless as Wilkins as he nodded to her and went across the beach and up to the house.

The following morning when Holly came down to the beach, there was no sign of Hubert. She got into her swim suit, because she had used it so much that now she felt it was hers, and practiced awhile. But when she saw Wilkins laying breakfast on the glass-enclosed terrace and came up, there was still no sign of Hubert. And only one place had been laid.

"Mr. Beardsley flew up to New York last night, miss," Wilkins explained. "Some sudden business call. He'll be gone several days, but he left word you were to 'carry on' just as though he were here. I'm to see to it that you have whatever you need while he is gone."

Holly thanked him around the sudden

lump in her throat and managed to eat breakfast. But she was relieved when he began clearing the table, and she walked down the beach.

She had found a place at the farthest end of the private beach, right at the very end where the huge groins thrust up to separate the private beach from the tangled, seaweed-and-driftwood-strewn public beach beyond. She had never seen anyone using that public beach. Above, along the road, a section had washed out during a bad hurricane a year or so ago and had never been repaired. Beyond this unkempt stretch of beach the tall dunes lifted their yellow shoulders.

Holly reached the spot where she always sat, her knees drawn up encircled by her arms, her face turned towards the great mass of ocean, incredibly blue, foam-laced where the great breakers rolled lazily in. She had wondered how it happened that whoever cleaned the Beardsley beach every morning had overlooked this big palm log that formed such an excellent back rest. Because of the condition of the public beach, she knew that the Beardsley beach would have been equally unkempt unless it was cleaned daily. And she had an absurd vision of a brace of cleaning women, armed with buckets and mops, out industriously scrubbing that beach — and laughed at the vision. It must be the gardeners who tended the beach, she supposed.

She was jerked out of her mixed-up thoughts by the sound of voices above her. A girl jumped over the lowest part of the fence of groins, followed by a second girl. They both stopped, startled, as they saw Holly.

"Oops!" said the first arrival, the salt-tangy wind tossing her ruddy curls above a charming, slightly freckled face, her lovely mouth curled in a grin. "We should have known, Connie, when we found this place, it was too good to be true! Let's get out before we're arrested for trespassing."

She turned back to go the way she

had come, but Holly had scrambled to her feet and held out a hand in eager protest.

"Oh, please don't go!" she begged.

The redhead turned, eyeing her above the pile of beach towels and essentials for sun-bathing that she carried. Her green eyes swept Holly from head to foot, and the lovely blonde who now stood on the lowest groin waited for these two to make up their minds. She was similarly laden with sun-bathing paraphernalia, and a terry-cloth beach robe was merely slung from her shoulders, revealing an exquisite young body in a brief blue swim suit just a shade deeper than the color of her eyes.

"Look," said the redhead carefully, "we knew perfectly well when we spotted this place a couple of weeks ago that it was a restricted area, a private beach. But we kept on using it. So if you want to call the cops go to it — though we'll go quietly, I promise — "

"So it's a private beach and belongs to the Beardsleys," Holly cut in, eager to keep these two girls only a few years older than herself. "But I'm sure Mr. Beardsley would be delighted to have you use it. He's awfully nice and very kind! So please stay. I'll go away, if you'd rather."

The two strangers exchanged puzzled glances and looked back at Holly.

"You're not trespassing, too, are you?" asked the redhead.

"Oh, no, I'm staying with the Beardsleys," Holly answered. "Mr. Beardsley's teaching me to swim, only now he's gone to New York — and I'd be so glad if you'd stay! I'm lonely."

The redhead and the blonde exchanged swift glances and then looked up and across at the beautiful villa. The redhead shrugged.

"Poor little rich girl, eh?" she commented dryly.

Holly laughed ruefully.

"Goodness, no! I'm nobody at all, really. I'm just here until the Lamonts can think what to do with me," she blurted out.

The redhead glanced at the blonde and raised her eyebrows slightly.

"I feel as if I'd come into a movie right in the middle, and will have to stay for the beginning to find out what it's all about," she said as she spread her gaily colored blanket, dropped her burden on it and sat down. "Tell us more! Oh, I'm Janet Wilkes, and this is my roommate, Connie Blake."

"How do you do?" said Holly politely, as Gran had always taught her. "I'm Holly Tolliver."

"Hi, Holly," said Janet. "You were saying?"

She had dropped her beach robe, and now she was rubbing sun-tan oil into her lovely arms and watching Holly curiously.

"So you're visiting the Beardsleys," she suggested.

Holly plunged into her brief story, and the two girls watched her curiously, as they attended to oiling their lovely bodies against the sun. When she had finished it was Janet who spoke, frowning slightly.

"But why didn't the old girl — pardon, why didn't your grandmother make provision for you in her will so you wouldn't have to wait for the Lamonts to do something about you?"

"Oh, Gran didn't leave a will," Holly explained. "She was — well, I suppose superstitious or something. She hated the idea of dying, and I suppose she felt if she made a will — "

"How old was she when she died?" asked Connie curiously.

"Ninety-one."

Janet whistled. "Then maybe not making a will isn't such a bad idea after all," she admitted, "though it does leave you in something of a spot. But I suppose out of gratitude to you for living with her and taking care of her all these years, the Lamonts will do the handsome thing by you. Where do the Beardsleys come into it, by the way?"

"Oh, Mrs. Beardsley was a Lamont

before she married," answered Holly. "And the Lamont men, Walker and Charles, aren't married, so they asked her to let me stay here until they could decide what should be done with me."

Janet glanced at Connie, who was listening, her blue eyes wide.

"Sounds like a rather nice set-up, wouldn't you say, Connie? Two young, unmarried men — they *are* young, Holly?" Janet remembered to ask.

"Oh, yes. Well, not really young," Holly answered. "I think Walker is about thirty and Charles is maybe a few years younger."

"*And* joint heirs to a fabulous estate. My girl, you're shot with luck! Beautiful as you are — " Janet began.

"Oh, golly, I'm not!" protested Holly, wide-eyed.

Janet's eyes swept her from head to foot, and Janet grinned.

"Well, from where I sit you're a darned good-looking girl," she insisted.

"They'll think of something, don't you fret!"

"I hope so," said Holly soberly. She added quickly, "Of course, it's nice here and Mr. Beardsley is kind and good, but — well, back at the Hacienda I had things to do. Here, I just sit — I get tired of just doing nothing."

"I should be so tired!" moaned Connie.

Holly looked at her eagerly.

"Do you have a job?" she asked wistfully.

"I'm executive secretary to one of the top men in the real estate game down here, and I'm sure you can imagine what *that* means. Never a dull moment," Connie admitted.

Janet chuckled. "Besides which, she's engaged to be married to a rising young attorney, and she's busy 'boning up' so she can be a real help to him when he hangs out his shingle and starts practicing on his own, instead of being a 'leg man' for one of the big outfits down here."

"It sounds wonderful." Holly could not keep the envy out of her voice. "Are you a private secretary, too, Janet?"

Janet shook her head, carefully stroking sun-tan oil into her lovely legs.

"Oh, no, I'm an airplane stewardess," she answered carelessly. "I fly the New York-Palm Beach run during the season."

She looked up, puzzled at Holly's exclamation and the expression of awe on her face, and straightened, staring at Holly.

"For Pete's sake, Holly!" she protested. "You look as if I'd said I was the first woman to penetrate outer space. What's so all-fired exciting about being an airline stewardess?"

"It must be very exciting and thrilling," Holly breathed.

Laughter touched Janet's green eyes.

"Oh, it's terribly thrilling," she mocked. "I stand at the door, all dressed up in my snappy uniform, and I say, 'Welcome aboard, sir' or

'Madam' as the case may be, and then I hold my breath and hope there won't be any crying babies. And I also hope that no one will be air-sick — and that the food that's just come aboard and which I shall soon be serving is palatable and will be accepted with appreciation. Oh, yes, it's a great thrill!"

"Stop sneering!" ordered Connie firmly. "You know darned well it's the only profession in the world you really love and that you've just about given up the idea of getting married because you know if you do, you'll be permanently grounded."

Janet laughed and wrinkled her faintly tip-tilted nose, across which a row of freckles marched gaily.

"Oh, well, it *is* fun at that," she conceded. "And I do love it."

Connie asked, "Where's your sun-tan oil, Holly? Did you forget it? Want to borrow mine?"

Janet said quickly, "With that gorgeous toast-brown tan she's got she doesn't need it. You really do have a lovely tan, Holly. I envy you."

Holly looked from friendly green eyes to friendly blue ones and said huskily, "And I envy you two for a whole lot more than just a nice tan."

Janet studied her for a moment, then smiled warmly and held out the suntan oil.

"Smear some on my back, will you, Holly? I like to look and smell like a well-dressed salad when I'm baking," she suggested lightly. Flushed and happy, Holly obeyed.

It was soon obvious that a day on the beach for Connie and Janet meant a brief swim and a long nap, and then lunch which they had brought with them. As Janet reached for the bag that held the lunch, Holly stood up awkwardly.

"I'd better be getting back to the cabaña," she said quickly. "Wilkins will be bringing my lunch there."

Janet cocked an eyebrow at her, and Connie said, a smothered giggle in her throat. "Don't look now, but there's a gent perambulating down the beach who looks as if his name couldn't possibly be anything but Wilkins — a 'gentleman's gentleman' if I ever saw one."

"Probably coming to give us the bum's rush, Connie me girl, so put those sandwiches back in the bag," said Janet ruefully.

"Oh, I'm sure he isn't," protested Holly, wondering unhappily if he was.

Wilkins came on, carefully carrying a rather splendid-looking basket. When he had reached them, he bowed to Holly and put the basket beside her.

"I took the liberty of bringing your lunch, Miss Holly, thinking you would probably enjoy having it with your friends," he said with his usual wooden expression, though his eyes flicked to Janet and Connie.

"Oh, thank you, Wilkins, that was very kind," said Holly eagerly. "These are my friends, Miss Wilkes and Miss Blake And this is my friend, Mr. Wilkins, Connie and Janet."

Before anyone could speak, she looked up, stricken, at Wilkins.

"I'm sorry, Wilkins, I forgot," she apologized, while Connie and Janet looked understandably puzzled.

Wilkins permitted himself a faint smile.

"It's quite all right, miss," he said, and bowed to the two girls.

"Wilkins, eh?" mused Janet, eyeing him curiously. "My name is Wilkes, but I don't imagine we are related, do you?"

Wilkins gave her an amused glance that almost destroyed his well-trained blankness, and bowed again.

"I am afraid not, miss, though I'm sorry to have to say so," he admitted, and was once more his formal self as he turned to Holly. "Will there be anything more, Miss Holly?"

"Nothing, Wilkins, thanks a lot!"

Wilkins included them all in his final bow, turned and marched back up the beach. Connie's and Janet's eyes followed him.

"So that's a 'gentleman's gentleman,'" commented Connie after a moment. "I never dreamed I'd live to see one, unless he was in a movie and played by David Niven, of course."

"He's quite a lad," Janet agreed, and once more her green eyes on Holly were quite thoughtful. "Somehow, I don't feel nearly as sorry for you as I did. Waited on hand and foot — "

"I'd much rather be back at the Hacienda waiting on Gran," Holly answered stubbornly. "Not that she ever let anybody wait on her much. She was always so proud of doing things for herself. She was a wonderful person."

"Here, what you need is food, my pet," Janet assured her briskly, and began exploring the contents of the basket Wilkins had brought.

When much later in the afternoon Connie and Janet began reluctantly preparing to leave the beach, Holly watched them, her mouth drooping wistfully. Suddenly Janet turned to her.

"Look, Holly, if it won't upset any of the arrangements at the Beardsley shack, why don't you come and have dinner with Connie and me?" she suggested.

Connie looked momentarily startled, and then echoed the invitation heartily.

Holly was enraptured. "Oh, could I?"

"If the Beardsleys won't mind?"

"Oh, they won't even miss me. Mr. Beardsley's gone to New York, and Mrs. Beardsley won't even know I'm not there," Holly said eagerly. "I'll run up and tell Mary so she won't bring me a dinner-tray, and I'll put on some clothes. Oh, are you *sure* you don't mind having me?"

Janet scowled.

"Would we have asked you if we minded? Scat now and get changed. We'll wait for you," Janet ordered, and Holly turned and fled.

5

U P on the road above the private beach a small blue sedan was parked. Janet unlocked the door, stuffed the beach paraphernalia into the back and slid beneath the wheel.

"It'll be a close fit, Holly." She grinned as Holly slid in beside her and made room for Connie. "But it's only a short haul. You won't be too bruised and battered by the time we get home. Was Mary willing to miss serving your dinner in your room?"

"Oh, I asked Wilkins to tell her. She was busy in the kitchen," said Holly happily.

"And was Wilkins willing for you to make friends so fast?"

"He was glad I'd met you both and hoped we'd have a nice time," answered Holly innocently.

The little car was scampering down Royal Palm Way. At Lake Drive it turned south past a row of stately, old-fashioned houses, some dating back almost to the days of the Florida boom. In front of one of these, Janet turned the car through the great stucco gateposts and along a shell-strewn drive, to halt beside a stately, rather gloomy-looking house built in the pseudo-Spanish style.

Wide-eyed, Holly gasped as she took in the beautifully kept shrubbery, the perfect lawn, the great flaming masses of bougainvillea that smothered the arches along the terrace. "Do you live here?"

Janet chuckled. "We live there," she answered, and indicated a capacious garage with room for half a dozen cars and an apartment above it. "Connie's firm handles the rental — or the sale, if anybody can be found dumb enough to buy a huge place like this nowadays — of the property. We are listed as etakers, and pay our rent by opening the place once or twice a week, seeing to it that there is no damage of wind, weather or hurricane."

"It looks very much like the Hacienda," Holly admitted as she slid out of the car and looked about her, sniffing. "I smell orange blossoms!"

"Why not? That's our breakfast," Connie laughed. "There are a few orange and grapefruit trees, and a couple of ponderosa lemons beyond the patio. We see they're kept in trim, too, and have all the fruit we can use."

Janet, carrying her share of the beach paraphernalia, led the way along the drive and to the outside stairs that led up to the apartment above the garage. The place was neatly but not luxuriously furnished, and the two girls had applied the expected feminine touches: bright colors, a few good flower prints, gaily patterned draperies — and the whole effect was cheerful and gay.

Holly was entranced both by

apartment and by the unaccustomed feminine companionship. While Connie disappeared into one of the two bedrooms to dress for her dinner date and while Janet was declining Holly's help in the small kitchen, she wandered happily about the place.

"Oh," she called to Janet delightedly, "you've got a portable typewriter. I've never used a portable. I tried to get Gran to buy one, but she insisted the old standard was good enough. I think it must have been one of the very first ones made, it was so different from the ones I used at school."

Janet popped her head in from the kitchen.

"You can use a typewriter?" she demanded.

"Well, of course." Holly was puzzled by the effect of her simple statement. "I used to write all Gran's letters for her. She wanted me to take the commercial course my last year in high. I learned to ᵘᵉ a dictaphone, but I was never much ᶜᵃ𝗻d at shorthand. The instructor said it wasn't important, since I could type and use the dictaphone."

Janet stared at her for a moment, a saucepan in one hand, a large mixing spoon in the other. Then she called, "Hi, Connie, she can type!"

Connie, settling the folds of a smart blue taffeta sheath about her slender body, answered from the bedroom doorway, "I heard her."

"So?" demanded Janet.

Holly looked from one to the other, puzzled.

"So what?" demanded Connie.

"What's the good of being an executive secretary if you can't throw a little weight around?" Janet wanted to know.

"Oh, good grief, Jan — " Connie was alarmed.

"So why not give the kid a break? She may be darned good."

Holly asked anxiously, "What *are* you two talking about?"

"Do you want a job?" Janet demanded.

Holly caught her breath and her eyes flew wide.

Connie made a slight, protesting gesture, and Janet frowned at her.

"A job?" Holly breathed, incredulous before the prospect. "Could I?"

Janet answered her by asking Connie, "Well? You said yourself you were going to have to put on some extra typists now that new sub-division has been approved for a loan. Why not give Holly a chance?"

Connie was obviously reluctant.

"Well, after all, Jan, she's had no experience."

"She handled the old lady's correspondence. She's had a commercial course at high school. And how's she going to get experience if nobody will give her a job?" Jan insisted.

Connie yielded, and whipped the cover off the machine. From a desk drawer she brought out a printed slip, slipped it into the typewriter and motioned to Holly.

"There's an application blank," she

said crisply. "Let's see you fill it out."

"Bear in mind, Connie me girl, that the machine's new to her," Janet warned.

"Bear in mind she's never worked before."

"And that she's barely old enough for a job."

The two studied each other, and Holly looked from one to the other, her fingers trembling a little as they rested on the keys. And then quickly she began filling in the blank spaces on the application form, while Janet and Connie watched her, Janet with glee, Connie with a lessening of her reluctance.

Holly looked up, frowning.

"It says here, 'References,'" she said uneasily.

"Put down Mr. Beardsley, Holly. His name carries considerable weight in these parts."

"Oh, does it?" asked Holly wonderingly.

"How naive can you be?" Janet

murmured, and Connie nodded.

"It does, indeed," Connie told Holly dryly, and Holly's fingers tapped out the name obediently.

Connie took the application form, studied it, and nodded.

"I'll file it with Personnel Monday morning," she promised.

"With a recommendation, I hope?" Janet pursued her relentlessly.

"Of course!" Connie snapped. "Now get off my back, will you?"

She disappeared into the bedroom and Janet grinned at Holly.

"You'll have a job, Holly, by the end of the week," she promised. "That is, if the Beardsleys will permit it."

"Oh, I'm sure they'll be glad to be rid of me," Holly answered quite honestly, and Janet's green eyes warmed with pity.

"And now let's see about dinner," she suggested briskly.

There was a rap at the door, and Janet opened it, calling out to Connie. "That man's here, Connie."

To the young man who came into the room, she said casually, "Hi, Jimmy. This is Holly."

"Hello, Holly," said the pleasant young man, smiling at her. Connie came into the room. Then he forgot everybody else. "Hi, honey, you look scrumptious as always. Ready?"

Connie tucked her hand through his arm and floated out of the room with him. Janet watched them go, and then she looked at Holly and nodded thoughtfully.

"There they go, on Cloud Nine," she murmured. "A couple of the nicest youngsters you'd ever want to meet and so desperately in love with each other that it's a little frightening."

Holly asked curiously, "Frightening to be so much in love?"

Janet's lovely brows were drawn together in a small frown.

"Being that much in love makes you so darned vulnerable," she said. "Me, I want no part of it. I like being *me*, and answerable to no one else! I don't like sitting by the telephone, aching with the fear that he won't call, dying a little every time he doesn't, and running to meet him with my heart held in my hands when he comes back."

She drew a hard breath, the slight frown faded, and she squared her shoulders, laughing at her own emotion.

"I sound like a very bad soap opera, don't I?" she grinned. "And that's pretty funny, because I loathe soap operas and I've never been in love in my life, and I'd like to keep it that way. Come on; let's have dinner."

It was a typical business girl's dinner, but to Holly, because it was eaten in pleasant, friendly companionship with a girl she was learning to like, nothing had ever been more delicious. And afterwards, when they had cleared the table and washed the dishes and talked for an hour or so, Janet said briskly, "I'd better get you back home before they send a posse out after you."

"I don't imagine anybody would miss me if I didn't show up for days,"

Holly confessed soberly.

"Oh, I'm sure Wilkins would," Janet chided her lightly as they went down to the drive, where the small foreign sedan was waiting patiently for them. "Hop in and I'll speed you on your way — that is, if Betsy is willing."

Apparently Betsy was, for the little car started immediately. As Janet drove down the Trail to Royal Palm Way and turned east toward Ocean Drive, a giant pumpkin-yellow moon was hanging above the dark, tumbled silk of the white-topped breakers.

"It's beautiful, isn't it?" she murmured. "And this has been the most wonderful evening. I'm so grateful to you and Connie, Janet — so very, very grateful."

"For what, I'd like to know, you ridiculous child?"

"For beings friends with me," Holly answered. "I've never had friends before. Oh, in school there were a few kids I knew fairly well. I never visited in their homes, and they never visited in mine. We just met at school. Sometimes Sam would be a little late coming for me, and I'd have time for a coke at the drug store with them. So you and Connie are the first two *real* friends I've ever had."

When they reached the corner above the Beardsley villa Janet whistled, for there were several cars parked outside and others rolling into the drive, disgorging evening-dressed women and their escorts. The whole lower floor of the villa was ablaze with lights and there was the sound of music, voices, laughter: all the sounds that indicate a party.

"I'll get out at the service entrance," Holly told Janet quietly, matter of factly.

"Oh, you will, will you?" Janet protested. "I'll drive you right up to the front entrance, you can barge right in, say, 'Evening, folks,' and join the party."

"Oh, golly!" Holly was appalled at the suggestion. "I wouldn't dare.

Mrs. Beardsley wouldn't like it. I'd much rather slip through the service entrance and up the side stairs to my room."

Janet's mouth was a thin, grim line as she proceeded down the side street to the service entrance, where Holly turned to her.

"It's been the very nicest evening I've ever known," she said quite honestly.

"You know something?" drawled Janet, smiling at her, though there wasn't a vestige of a smile in her voice. "I have a strong suspicion that this is just the first of a whole lot of evenings like this. I'll see you the last of the week, back on the beach. I have two days off down here between flights and then twenty-four hours off in New York. I'm flying out tomorrow, but I'll see you when I get back."

"I'll be looking forward to it," Holly said eagerly. She added a good night, slipped along the narrow service entrance and was swallowed up in the shadows.

Janet sat where she was for a moment. Then, her jaw set in a grim line, she started the little car and went driving off down the road and through to Royal Palm Way, her thoughts very busy.

6

THOUGH she had walked to the end of the beach where she had first met Connie and Janet every morning since that first morning, it was not until Thursday that Holly saw Janet waiting for her. She gave a little childish whoop of delight and raced the last few yards. Janet laughed at the exuberance of her greeting, touched by the girl's warm delight.

"I thought maybe you weren't coming back," Holly confessed.

"What? And give up the chance to loll on a private beach like this?" Janet grinned. "Take a look at the one beyond, that's free to the public — though I admit I can't see what right even the Beardsleys have to shut off a whole section of the Atlantic and say no one else must use it. But sit down, youngster. I've got some news for you."

Happily Holly dropped on the sand and waited, an eager expectancy in her eyes.

"It's about that job Connie and I promised you," Janet told her. "It's yours, and you can start work Monday morning, if you still want it."

Holly stared at her, round-eyed, breathless.

"Well, for Pete's sake," Janet protested, "I'm not offering you a mortgage on the moon and a trip around the world. I'm only offering you a job — rather, Connie is. It'll be dull, hard work, and it doesn't pay a whole heck of a lot, but it *will* give you some business experience. It's only temporary — just until the end of the season — about the last of March."

"Oh, Jan, Jan — do you really mean it? A job?"

"Of course I mean it, you blessed idiot," said Janet, laughing. "If the Beardsleys agree — "

"Oh, I'm sure they will!"

"The salary isn't much. But Connie and I thought that if you didn't want to stay on here you could move in with us, until you get your feet on the ground and decide whether you like it."

"I'll love it," Holly told her swiftly, "if it won't crowd you and Connie. And, of course, I'd want to pay my share of expenses — "

"Of course." Janet dismissed that, and went on, "Of course, too, you have to tell the Beardsleys about it, and if they disapprove — "

"They won't! They'll be relieved to be rid of me."

"Even Papa Beardsley?" Janet mocked curiously.

"Oh, I don't think he'll mind," Holly answered earnestly. "He's been kind and sweet. But I know he'll want me to do whatever I want to do."

Janet said crisply, "Look, infant, you don't know one blessed thing about Connie and me — and yet you're willing to jump out of that big place back there and move in with us? How do you know what sort of girls we are? You could be stepping into a pretty nasty mess. Honestly, Holly, I didn't know they *grew* girls as innocent as you are!"

Holly stared at her, puzzled, secretly hurt.

"I know you and Connie are wonderful," she began.

"You don't know a darned thing about us! We've *told* you things — but you haven't the faintest idea whether they are true or not," Janet protested with heat. "So you have a talk with Papa Beardsley. Bring him to meet Connie and me, let him see where you'll be living, let him investigate us — and believe me, if he doesn't — well, then he's as bad as all the rest of that gang."

"I don't know what you're mad about," Holly said.

"You idiot! I'm not 'mad.' Haven't you heard? Only dogs get mad. People get irritated! And I'm irritated because you're so darned innocent and unsuspicious — and it's a dangerous way to be in the kind of world we live in these days!" Janet told her sharply. "So talk to Beardsley, tell him what's up and see what he says. Connie and I will be here Saturday morning, unless he gets back from New York and wants to come to the apartment to investigate us."

She stood up, gave Holly a little wave and went back up the beach.

She sighed and went forlornly back to the villa.

In the morning when she came down to the cabaña, Hubert was there, and she raced to greet him as joyously as she had greeted Janet yesterday, a fact that Hubert seemed to find pleasing.

"And what have you been up to while I was gone?" Hubert asked as they sipped iced papaya juice.

It all tumbled out in a spate of words that Hubert at first had some difficulty in following. When she had finished the story, he put down the half-finished juice and looked up at Wilkins.

"You've met the young ladies, Wilkins?" he asked.

"Oh, yes, sir. Very nice young ladies, they seem, sir."

The two men exchanged level-eyed glances, and Holly looked from one to the other, held in suspense.

"Oh, please, Mr. Beardsley, may I?" Holly pleaded when it seemed that the silence between the men was not going to end.

Startled by the urgency of her plea, Hubert frowned at her.

"It means so much to you, Holly, to get away from here?" he asked.

Color poured into Holly's face, but she met his eyes straightforwardly.

"Yes," she answered with a desperate sincerity. "Oh, you've been very kind and I'm grateful, and Wilkins and Mary, too. But just think, a job of my own — I'll be self-supporting. Connie and Jan are darlings, and their apartment is plenty big enough for us all. Oh, please."

"If you want it that much, Holly,"
said Hubert, and his tone made Wilkins
look at him with sudden curiosity. "But
of course I'll have to meet these young
ladies. I must be quite sure about the
place you're going to live and the girls
with whom you're going to live."

Holly said, "Jan said you'd want
to — or she wouldn't think much
of you."

For a moment there was a spark of
amusement in Hubert's eyes.

"Oh, she did, did she? She sounds
like quite a girl," he admitted. "Do
you think she's on the beach this
morning?"

"She said she and Connie would
come back Saturday. But this is her day
off, and she'll be at the apartment,"
Holly answered eagerly.

"Then suppose we go see her, shall
we?" Hubert stood up.

"Now?"

"Why not, if you want to start your
job Monday?"

Holly was on her feet, eyes shining.

She thanked him and then raced up to the beach stairs.

Hubert accepted a second cup of coffee and looked up at Wilkins.

"You thought them acceptable, Wilkins?" he asked at last.

"Very much so, sir. If I may say so, they seemed excellent friends for Miss Holly, who needs young feminine friends, don't you think, sir?"

"I do, indeed, Wilkins, and thanks," said Hubert.

Holly had donned the inevitable navy blue and was running a comb through her cap of sloe-black curls when Mary tapped at the door, her eyes big.

"The master is waiting for you, Miss Holly, in the front hall," Mary announced, obviously astounded that such a thing was possible.

"Oh, thanks, Mary. Oh, something wonderful is about to happen, Mary." Holly brushed past the girl and down the corridor to the front stairs.

Mary watched her, big-eyed, and murmured under her breath, "Well, forevermore — who'd ever have thought it? What's the crack about 'still waters running deep'? Believe me, they sure do."

Hubert turned as Holly came racing down the stairs and guided her through a wide open front door, guarded by a neatly uniformed houseman who had difficulty keeping his well-trained features in order.

Hubert's roadster, a long, sleek monster of black and silver, was waiting in the drive, and the head chauffeur held the door open as Hubert guided Holly into it and swung the door shut.

As Hubert slid beneath the wheel and started the car, the head chauffeur stood back. The houseman came down the steps, and the head-gardener came up. The three middle-aged men eyed each other, and then the drive down which Hubert and Holly had vanished.

It was the head chauffeur who broke the taut silence.

"Well, like I say, you never can tell."

"Well, she's a cute kid — even if she is kinda simple," offered the houseman.

"I just hope Madam is sleeping late as usual and didn't look out of her window." The gardener grinned significantly.

"That will be quite enough," said the houseman stiffly, but his eyes were twinkling wickedly as he turned and went back into the house.

Following Holly's excited directions, Hubert turned into the Trail and slowed, as she said eagerly, "There it is."

Hubert stared at the big gray-stone house, half-smothered in bougainvillea and hibiscus, and frowned down at Holly.

"Why, this is the old Peralta place," he said. "Your friends must be very successful career girls indeed if they can afford a place like this."

Holly laughed. "Oh, they live in the garage apartment," she answered. "The firm Connie works for handles the estate, and Connie and Jan act as caretakers and get a reduced rent on the apartment."

"Oh, so that's it." Hubert seemed oddly relieved as he drove between the gray stone gateposts and along the drive to the garage.

Jan, clad in blue slacks and a thin shirt, was coming down the outside stairs, carrying a laundry basket heaped with wet clothes. She paused and smiled as she recognized Holly and looked curiously at Hubert.

"Jan, this is Mr. Beardsley." Holly jumped out of the car and ran towards her. "And, Mr. Beardsley, this is my friend, Miss Wilkes."

Jan's green eyes held a small twinkle as she put a damp hand in the one Hubert extended.

"Of course it is," she answered, and said lightly, "Welcome aboard, Mr. Beardsley, I hope you will have a pleasant flight."

Momentarily puzzled, Hubert's expression altered as he recognized her. "But of course, now I remember. You were the hostess on the flight that brought me down last night. You look quite different."

"I should hope so," laughed Jan. "The airline would fire me pronto if I tried to get aboard like this. But career girls have laundry to do, no matter how high they may fly on their jobs."

"Jan, let me hang out the laundry while you talk to Mr. Beardsley," begged Holly, as though she asked for some special boon. "You'll want to talk about me — and maybe you'd rather I wasn't around."

"Well, we can discuss you a little more mercilessly if you aren't present," Jan agreed, smiling as she surrendered the basket. "Will you come this way, Mr. Beardsley?"

She led the way back up the stairs, and Hubert caught the imploring, anxious look in Holly's eyes as she lifted the basket and moved toward the drying yard at the back of the apartment.

Jan stood at the open door of the apartment and motioned Hubert inside. She saw him look swiftly about the place while she leaned against the closed door, waiting, an enigmatic smile on her piquant face.

"Very nice," said Hubert, turning to face her. "And it's very kind of you and your friend to want to look after Holly."

"It's time somebody did, don't you think?"

Hubert stiffened slightly.

"I beg your pardon?" His tone registered his resentment.

"Oh, I know from what she tells me that you have been kind to her, Mr. Beardsley, and I'm very glad," Jan told him quietly. "But picking her up by the scruff of the neck, dragging her out of the only home she has ever known and plumping her down in the servants' quarters while you make up your mind what to do with her seems pretty rough treatment for a girl like Holly, don't you think?"

"As a matter of fact, I couldn't agree with you more," Hubert told her so frankly that he took her by surprise. "But of course the whole thing is a Lamont project and — since I'm not a Lamont — well, I did what I could, but it wasn't nearly enough."

"Holly's a darling, but she's almost criminally innocent, Mr. Beardsley, even dangerously ignorant," Jan told him with a frankness that matched his own. "In the world as it is nowadays, innocence and ignorance are not sufficient protection for young and lovely girls — as I'm sure you will agree."

"I do, of course, and the fact has, I may as well admit, bothered me." Hubert nodded. "And you think by getting her a job, bringing her here to live, you can remedy her ignorance and her innocence?"

Jan gave him a sharp glance.

"Working in a big office with twenty or more girls her own age or a little older, where there are a good many young men to provide her with dates and entertainment, will teach her to stand on her own feet and open her eyes to the world outside the shell in which she has been brought up. All this, of course, providing you and the Lamonts agree to trust her with us," she said levelly.

Hubert had listened to her intently, his eyes meeting her own straightly.

"You must realize, Miss Wilkes, that all this is a surprise to me," he began with an unaccustomed awkwardness.

Jan smiled. "You want references from both Connie and me, to assure you Holly will be in quite safe hands," she answered. "We'll be happy to supply them, and we'd be unwilling to have Holly here unless you had checked those references carefully. After all, you know nothing about us. We could easily be a couple of very unsavory characters with evil designs on Holly."

Hubert laughed, "I could hardly think that, now that I've met you. And knowing the very high standards the airlines demand of their hostesses — "

"Stewardesses, Mr. Beardsley," Jan mocked him lightly.

"There is one thing, Miss Wilkes, that puzzles me a lot," Hubert admitted frankly. "Why should you want to — to take on the responsibility of a girl like Holly? It *is* a responsibility, you know."

Jan left the door and dropped into a chair, her eyes thoughtful.

Hubert sat opposite her, and when she reached for a cigarette he leaned forward and offered a light. She nodded her thanks as she relaxed. A small, thoughtful frown creased her brow, and for a moment she was silent. And then she raised her eyes and met his, and the frown deepened.

"I'll have to admit, Mr. Beardsley, that's what Connie wanted to know," she said quite simply. "I don't quite understand it myself, except that I've always had a great deal of sympathy for the underdog."

Hubert's jaw hardened slightly.

"And you think of Holly as the underdog?"

Jan smiled thinly. "Let's just say she's the girl outside your family circle; outside just about everything that could make her happy."

"And you think she would be happy here, working with your friend?"

"Don't you?"

Hubert turned the thought over in his mind, looking about the pleasant, unpretentious place that had a cozy hominess about it that was appealing.

"I imagine she will be," he agreed. "But it's more than a stranger should be called on to do for her. You really are strangers, you know."

Jan leaned forward and scrubbed out her cigarette, her eyes on the heavy glass ash tray.

"My father died when I was seven," she said quietly, and for a moment Hubert found it difficult to follow her. "My mother and I went to live with my grandmother. She had always disliked my father and had opposed my mother's marriage so when we had to come to live with her, she wasn't overly kind. I'd always had pets. I loved animals; the smaller, the more helpless the more I loved them. But she hated animals. I found a kitten once, a tiny scrap of a thing that had been abandoned and was weak from hunger and terrified of its small life. I took it home. My grandmother refused to let me keep it; she wouldn't even let me feed it. She paid a garbage man to destroy it — before my eyes."

Hubert studied her, and knew that she had forgotten for the moment that he was there. She turned the ash tray between her fingers, and after a moment, she went on in that level, quiet voice.

"I've never forgotten that, or the way the kitten clung to me, or how little and soft it was and how pitifully it mewed." She broke off as though she had suddenly remembered his presence and looked up at him, color pouring into her face. "What a stupid, silly

thing for me to be saying, Mr. Beardsley
— practically giving you the story of
my life."

"You haven't been, at all. You've
given me the perfect reason for your
wanting to befriend Holly," said Hubert
swiftly. "She *is* something like a small,
lost kitten. The girl is outside all the
fun and good times that girls her age
should have. And I think she is very
lucky that she should have met you."

Jan asked, "Then you are willing for
her to come and live with us, and take
the job Connie has for her?"

"I'm more than willing, Miss Wilkes;
I'm delighted for her! And very grateful
to you and your friend. When may she
come?"

"Oh, the sooner the better, don't
you think?" Jan glowed happily. "I'll
be home today and tomorrow. Connie
will be here during the weekend, and
we can get her settled in so she will be
ready to start her new job Monday."

Hubert stood up, offered his hand,
gave hers a firm, friendly grip and said,

"Then I'll take her back to the villa so she can get packed. She will be back this afternoon, if that's all right with you?"

"That's perfect. But you won't have time to check references."

"Do you think I'd need to, *now*?"

Jan smiled and said quietly, "Thank you."

7

MARY was putting Holly's room to rights when Holly flew in like a small whirlwind, eyes shining, flushed and eager.

"Oh, Mary, I'm moving!" She laughed and tugged the ancient suitcase out of the small closet.

"Do tell!" mocked Mary, cold-eyed.

Something in her voice jerked Holly about to face her. Mary was eyeing her with a concentrated dislike so foreign to her usual warm friendliness that Holly's heart skipped a beat.

"Why, Mary, what's wrong?" she asked, bewildered.

"You're a foxy one, all right, I give you credit for that." Mary's tone was dry and inimical. "Though I suppose all of us should have had brains enough to know what's been going on between you and the master all along. Breakfasts in the cabaña, hours on the beach — and now he's moving you into your own apartment! I'm a fool to be surprised — and I'm not, really."

"Why, Mary, I don't know what you're talking about," said Holly.

"Like fun you don't!" Mary sneered. "If the Madam finds out, she'll snatch you bald, my girl — and who's to keep her from finding out, the way you and him are carrying on?"

"Mary, I've got a job, and I'm going to share an apartment with two girl friends. Mr. Beardsley has checked and is sure it will be quite all right. I mean — Mary, why are you looking at me like that?" Holly wailed.

"And you that was so wide-eyed and innocent butter wouldn't melt in your mouth — " Mary sneered.

There was a knock on the door, and it swung open to admit Hubert; Wilkins hovered helpfully in the rear.

Hubert glanced at Mary, who immediately became very busy, and then spoke to Holly. "Getting all packed? Need any help?"

"Oh, no, thanks," said Holly, and turned sharply away to conceal the shamed tears she could not control.

"Why, Holly, what's the matter?" protested Hubert. Mary tried to slip out of the room, but Wilkins blocked her way, eyeing her with a look that made Mary quail. "Don't you want to go? You needn't if you don't want to. I thought it was what you wanted."

"It is," Holly replied, tears thickening her voice as she crammed her few belongings into the case and snapped the lid shut.

She stood up, facing him, smiling despite the tears, her soft mouth tremulous.

"I'm all ready," she told him, so carefully avoiding a glance in Mary's direction that Hubert turned to Mary, his eyes stern.

"What have you been saying to her?" he demanded sharply.

Mary quailed, and then her head went up and her eyes flashed.

"Only what any decent, self-respecting girl would say to the likes of her," she snapped hotly. "Coming here, so shy and sweet and scared of her own shadow — and now running off with you to an apartment you've rented for her."

For a moment Hubert had to fight the impulse to slap the girl. She sensed the impulse and drew back, and the sudden fear in her eyes was a cold hand on his fury.

"You may go, Mary," he said through his teeth.

Mary flounced past him, and Wilkins drew aside, his eyes dark with displeasure, to allow her to pass.

For a moment there was a taut silence between the three who were left, and then Hubert said quietly, "You mustn't mind Mary, honey. She's just spiteful and malicious."

"Please," said Holly huskily, tugging at the handle of the suitcase, "I'd like to go."

"Of course, honey," said Hubert

gently, and added, "Do you have any money?"

"Oh, yes, I've got almost ten dollars."

Hubert brought his wallet out, drew out a sheaf of bills and held them out to her. But she drew back, refusing to touch them, her eyes wide and frightened.

"Now, Holly, be sensible," Hubert coaxed her, his mind seething with anger against Mary even while he realized that no doubt the rest of the servants shared her cynical suspicions. "It's only a hundred dollars. You'll need new clothes if you're going to be a business-girl, and if it bothers you, I'll let you pay me back after you start drawing a salary. Jan and Connie have their living to earn, and you must be able to pay your share, so you must take this money and use it. They'll help you shop; if you need more, just let me know."

Reluctantly Holly accepted the money and, without looking at it, thrust it into her shabby bag, her face turned away from Hubert.

"Wilkins, suppose you drive Miss Tolliver to her friends' place," said Hubert quietly, and handed over his keys. "It's the old Peralta place on Lake Trail. I shall be rather busy here for a while."

"Very good, sir," said Wilkins. He accepted the keys and Holly's ancient bag and went out of the room.

Holly hesitated, looking up at Hubert, and her voice shook as she said softly, "I don't know how to thank you."

"By being very happy in this new life, Holly, that's all I ask," Hubert answered. Impelled by an impulse he did not stop to analyze, he kissed her cheek lightly, smiling at her.

Holly's hand flew up to touch her cheek and her eyes widened. Then she turned toward the terrace, intent on escaping the route she always took to the beach.

"Wait, Holly," Hubert laid a restraining hand on her arm and turned her about towards the front stairs. "You are never to use the rear entrance again, Holly. Do you hear?"

"Thank you, but I'd rather," Holly said, broke free of him and ran down the corridor and through the door that led to the stairs. She had to circle the house to reach the front drive, and when she did, Wilkins was waiting for her, looking startled as she came from the back.

She got into the car with him, and Wilkins drove away . . .

Hubert was in the library some time later when the message for which he had been waiting came to him. He rose, smiling wryly as he went up the stairs and to his wife's door. Punctiliously he knocked and waited for her middle-aged, severe-looking maid to admit him, and to slip past him and away down the corridor as he entered the room.

Caro sat up in bed, surrounded by pastel-colored satin cushions, as carefully and deftly made up as though she had been ready for a fashion show.

Her hair was smoothly brushed and held back from her lovely face with a ribbon that matched the color of the rosy bed-jacket around her shoulders. But Hubert saw the ugliness of fury in her eyes that detracted considerably from the carefully managed picture she and her maid had set up.

Hubert his hands jammed into his pockets, stood eyeing her, waiting for her to break the silence between them.

"Well?" Caro snapped at last when it was obvious that he was not going to be the first to speak.

Hubert raised his eyebrows in a look of polite surprise.

"I believe you sent for me, my dear. You must have had something you wanted to tell me?" he suggested, coolly polite.

"I should think *you'd* have something to tell me," she snapped hotly.

"Oh?" still politely surprised. "Such as what?"

"Such as what's been going on between you and that — that — "

She caught back the word in time, drew a deep breath and went on, "I understand Holly has gone."

"Yes, I believe she has — " He smiled and added, "I'm surprised you even remembered she was here."

"Mathilda told me — " Now it was her turn to break off, and for a moment she watched him, her teeth sunk hard in her lower lip. "She told me, too, that your affair with Holly has become a scandal among the servants."

"Really?" his tone was mocking, but there was a dawning anger in his eyes.

"You must know that servants gossip among themselves, and among other servants. The whole story will be all over town — "

"And that worries you?" The mockery had deepened, and the look in his eyes was curious as he studied her, and she had the absurd feeling that he was seeing her in a light that was completely new to him, and utterly foreign to the way she wanted him to see her.

"Worries me? Of course it worries me," she flung at him furiously. "Why wouldn't it? I will not be gossiped about! Holly will have to come back here."

"I think not!"

Her face was convulsed with fury, her eyes blazing.

"Oh, don't think I don't know about the way you've been spending hours with her at the cabaña. I haven't said anything because I knew as long as you kept her here, there wouldn't be any real gossip. But now that you've taken an apartment for her — "

"She is sharing an apartment with a couple of friends, and she has a job."

"That's ridiculous! She has no friends, and how could she possibly get a job? She's had no training — or did you take care of that, too?"

The implication was so savage, so brutal that the mockery vanished from his eyes and they blazed with a fury that matched her own. His jaw was set and hard so that small white lines made parentheses that framed his tight-lipped mouth.

"I think you must really be out of your mind, Caroline," he told her in a voice he had used to her only a very few times in their life together and that always presaged real trouble between them. "Holly is a young and lovely girl — "

"I am a man old enough to be her father," Hubert went on as though she had not spoken. "Your insult to her is unforgivable, and your lack of faith in me is something I shan't forget. Would you like a divorce?"

The word rocked Caro as nothing he had ever said before had done.

She stared at him, eyes enormous, her face paling beneath the deft make-up.

"Because if you would, Caro, I'll consult my attorneys today," he finished.

Frightened by the deadly quiet of his voice, the monstrous thing he had said, and knowing so well that he was not one to make idle threats, she fought for some control over her helpless fury. But it was a long moment before she succeeded enough to answer him.

"Don't be ridiculous, Hubert," she said thinly. "You know I don't want a divorce — the idea is horrible. It's just that Holly must come back here because I promised Walker I would keep her here until we could decide what to do with her."

"Well, that decision is no longer yours, so you needn't trouble yourselves." Hubert was still speaking in that deadly quiet voice that sent little feathers of apprehension along her spine and deepened her hatred for Holly. "Two young women whom she met on the beach have taken her into their apartment, and one of them has found her a job. It seems that she is an excellent typist, by the way."

"She never told us that."

"I don't imagine you ever asked her whether she had any qualifications for a job of any kind," Hubert reminded her tautly. "But there is no point in prolonging this discussion, Caro. The problem of Holly has been solved, so you and your brothers needn't bother. Just forget the girl ever existed. I'm sure that won't be difficult."

He turned toward the door, but Caro's voice stopped him.

"Can *you* forget she ever existed, Hubert," she asked spitefully.

He looked back at her, and now there was contempt in his eyes.

"I'm afraid not, Caro — but don't let that trouble you. We were friends, nothing more."

"Hubert, will you swear that?" she demanded rashly.

His eyesbrows went up, and now the contempt had deepened in his eyes.

"Why, no, Caro, I don't think I will," he told her coolly. "You and I haven't had much of a marriage these last few years, but whether you wish to believe it or not, I have never been unfaithful to you."

"Nor I to you!" Caro flung at him.

"Oh, I'm quite sure of that." Hubert's

smile was thinlipped. "You're much too formal, too coolly aware of being Mrs. Hubert Beardsley with all the rights and appurtenances that goes with the title to risk losing it with an — shall we say indiscretion?"

And before she could recover from the outrageousness of that, the door had closed behind him.

8

HOLLY slid into the new life with an ease and a delight that made Connie and Jan feel very gentle toward her.

"She acts like a slum child going to the circus for the first time," Connie told Jan one evening when Holly had departed for her first date.

"That boy she's dating tonight — are you sure he will know how to behave himself?" demanded Jan.

Connie stared at her and dissolved in laughter.

"Oh, yessum, Gran'ma Jan, he's a real nice boy," she mocked. "He's the third one this week that's asked her for a date — and nearly scared her to death. I had to take strong measures to make her accept this invitation. It's for a movie and a soda afterwards, and he's promised to bring her straight home not later than ten-thirty."

Jan grinned ruefuly.

"Well, Papa Beardsley warned me we were taking on a great responsibility," she began.

Connie, dressing to go out on a date with her fiancé, burst out impatiently, "Oh, for Pete's sake, Jan, we can't let her be a millstone around our neck. Sure, she's a nice kid and I'm fond of her — but you can't expect to police her every move! Migosh, the kid's got to grow up sometime — why not stand aside and let her learn to walk by herself?"

Jan nodded reluctantly.

"Of course. You're right, Connie. It's just that she's so darned young!"

"She'll be nineteen come March, and I'm twenty-two and you're twenty-four," Connie pointed out logically. "And after all, being young isn't incurable."

"Falling in love with the wrong man *could* be."

There was the sound of a car

horn from the street and Connie said hurriedly, "There's my beloved. Why not take an aspirin and go to bed, Jannie darling? You're getting a nice mess of the colli-wobbles, and on you they don't look good."

She flashed out of the apartment.

She began briskly clearing away the dinner dishes, and had just washed and dried the last of them when she heard footsteps on the stairs and a brisk rapping at the door.

She swung it open and looked at the tall, good-looking young man who stood there.

"I'm Walker Lamont." He smiled pleasantly. "I'm looking for a girl named Tolliver."

Jan stiffened, and her eyes chilled as they swept over him.

"Are you now?" Her voice was deliberately mocking. "She's out."

"Will she be back soon?" Walker asked, puzzled by her hostility. "I don't want to seem insistent, but I really have to see her. I'm flying back to New York in the morning, and this will be my only chance to see her."

"And what did you want to see her about, Mr. Lamont?"

Puzzled, resentful of her deliberate hostility, Walker's own eyes chilled.

"I have to be quite sure that she is all right."

"Your solicitude seems to a bit tardy, Mr. Lamont, but very touching."

Walker's eyes swept over her: a slender, good-looking girl in blue slacks and a white shirt, her hair a copper-colored flame above her sea-green eyes and her faintly tip-tilted nose.

"I take it you're Miss — the airline stewardess," he said after a moment.

"Right. Holly's friend, I like to think. And believe me, I've seldom known a girl more in need of friends."

"Now, see here, Miss — whatever your name is — "

"It's Wilkes, Mr. Lamont, and I suppose you may as well come in." Jan stood back and motioned him to enter. "We can't very well stand here in the open doorway flinging insults at each other."

"I have no intention of flinging insults at you, Miss Wilkes, and frankly, I can't see why you should wish to fling them at me," Walker told her, as he walked into the living room and shot a swift glance about its pleasantly homey atmosphere. "I think it is quite understandable that I should feel a certain anxiety about Holly's welfare."

"Like I said before, Mr. Lamont, that's a bit tardy, don't you think? You picked her up by the scruff of the neck, like a stray kitten, plopped her down in the servants' wing of your sister's palatial abode, and then forgot all about her. You didn't mind in the least if she died of loneliness."

"We were trying to plan something for her."

"And the obvious plan, right under your nose, was too expensive?"

Puzzled, Walker said, "I don't get that."

"She had lived all her life at that Hacienda place, the last sixteen years looking after your great-grandmother," Jan pointed out. "Didn't it occur to you just to leave her there, where she was happy and had things to do to keep her occupied?"

"A young girl like Holly alone in a place like that?"

"But of course," Jan ignored his words, "you and your brother and sister had to sell the place because you needed the money so desperately."

"That's not true. Why, the check for the place after taxes was less than twenty thousand."

"Which would have sent Holly to a good training school where she could have learned a profession."

Walker said quietly, "This sort of thing is getting us nowhere. I've come from my sister's place, where she and I discussed Holly, and I want only to know that she is happy here, that she is contented."

"You may take my word for that."

"Sorry. I'll take Holly's word and no other."

To his angry amazement, Jan tipped back her copper-colored head and laughed in satirical amusement.

"I don't see anything so funny — " he began.

Eyes brimming with amusement, Jan studied him.

"That's because you can't see yourself as I see you, Mr. Lamont. To me, you are hilarious — in a repellent kind of way," she mocked him. "So terribly concerned now that Holly is no longer in a servant's room at your sister's, afraid to use the front entrance, lurking on the beach all day, dependent for whatever friendly gestures may come her way from a chambermaid — though she tells me Mr. Beardsley was very kind."

Walker nodded grimly.

"So my sister tells me," he answered with such heavy significance that for a moment Jan could only stare at him, while Walker waited for the full significance of his remark to sink in.

"Why, you unspeakable creature!" Jan gasped. "Are you trying to say your precious sister — why, what a fool she must be!"

"I understand Hubert offered my sister a divorce," said Walker grimly. "He'd hardly have done that if his interest in Holly hadn't been — shall we say, somewhat less than paternal?"

For a moment Jan was speechless with fury.

"So you can see," Walker went grimly on, "why I have to talk to Holly. My sister telephoned me, and I came down. Since I am chiefly responsible for Holly's being in her home, she felt that it was up to me to see what could be done."

Jan drew a deep, hard breath, her hands clenched tightly, and slowly counted to ten before she spoke.

"And what does Mr. Beardsley say about the affair?"

"Oh, he refuses to discuss it of course. Practically ordered me out of the house for even trying to talk to him."

"Well, bully for him! I admire his restraint for not kicking you out!"

"Now, see here — " Walker began, his temper slipping its leash.

"No, *you* see here!" blazed Jan. "If you could all know Holly — "

"That's just the point. None of us know her — except Hubert."

"I see," said Jan thoughtfully, studying him rather as though he had been something repulsive that she had accidentally turned up on the beach. "So now you've decided that it's time for you to get to know her, so you can drag her up by the roots again and plop her back into the servants' quarters."

"Nothing of the kind! The last thing in the world Caro or I want is for her to be returned to the villa or to be in touch with Hubert at all," Walker protested sharply.

"Then why are you here?"

Walker hesitated, and his eyes could

not quite meet that emerald-green, hostile gaze.

"Well, I'd like to be quite sure that she is happy here," he said finally.

"What you really mean and haven't the guts to say is that you want to be quite sure she is offering no threat to your sister's marriage."

Walker's jaw was set and hard, his eyes dark with anger.

"Considering that it was my fault Holly came in contact with Hubert at all — and I assure you my brother-in-law had never looked sideways at another woman until Holly came along — " Walker made a little gesture. "I'm sure you can see why I feel a certain responsibility for what's happened."

"You blazing idiot!" Jan's temper matched her hair. She had been struggling long enough to control it, and now she had lost it. "Nothing has happened except that one of your stuffed-shirt blue-bloods has offered a bit of well-meant kindness to a girl who was desperately in need of just such kindness! People like you make me sick!"

"Now wait a minute — "

"Connie and I met the child — because that's what she really is — on the beach." Jan was trying very hard to speak quietly. "She didn't realize how pathetic her small story was. She wasn't sorry for herself; she was just bewildered at the way things had happened. She was grieving for the old lady; she was lost and forlorn and humbly grateful to Mr. Beardsley when he condescended to notice her. And now you and that sister of yours are trying to make something ugly of the fact that he was kind to her!"

Walker said grimly, "If all that is true, then why did he mention divorce?"

"You should be able to answer that better than I. After all, I've never met your sister."

Walker straightened and eyed her with cold dislike.

120

"This seems to me a very pointless discussion."

"Discussion?" Jan was sweetly insolent. "I thought we were fighting. I was, anyway, because it's always been a pleasure to me to be able to be sassy to the likes of you, and I've met enough of the likes of you in my job to make me want to resign from the human race, if it wasn't for occasionally meeting people like Holly and Mr. Beardsley."

"I think," said Walker thoughtfully, "that you are one of the most unpleasant young women I've ever met."

"Why, thanks," Jan purred sweetly.

"You're quite beautiful, of course, and you are thoroughly aware of it, which gives you license, you feel, to be as unpleasant as you like."

There was the sound of a car in the drive below, light laughter, and then footsteps on the outside stairs.

Jan and Walker turned as the door opened and Holly came in, flushed, bright-eyed, very pretty in the yellow cotton frock Connie and Jan had helped her select. She saw Jan, but Walker was at one side of the room and she was unaware of him at first.

"Oh, Jan, darling, I'm so glad you and Connie insisted on my going with Hal," she said gaily. "I had such fun."

She turned and saw Walker, and the laughter and happiness were wiped out of her face instantly. She stiffened, and her eyes widened, and she took a backward step.

"No, no, I won't go back there. I won't, I won't!" she whimpered like a frightened child.

"Don't be afraid, honey. You don't have to go anywhere you don't want to go," Jan assured her firmly.

"I only wanted to see you, Holly, to decide if you were quite happy," Walker began, furious at the girl's terror.

"What he really wants to ask you, honey, is whether or not you are in love with Hubert Beardsley," said Jan sweetly.

It was obvious the question rocked Holly so that she stared incredulously from Jan to Walker, too stunned to answer. Walker said curtly, "The real question is whether Hubert is in love with you, Holly."

Holly stared at him, her eyes enormous in her pale face.

"Why, how could he be? He's married," she gasped at last.

Jan grinned impudently at Walker.

"In Lamont circles, honey, that's not always an adequate answer."

"Oh, be quiet." Walker flung the words at her so sharply that Jan blinked as he turned back to Holly. "Caro and Hubert have quarreled about his interest in you."

"But that's silly!" Holly protested, and added hotly, "Caro — I mean Mrs. Beardsley — is a very beautiful woman, and they have two children, and they've been married for ages, and he's old!"

"Convinced?" Jan mocked Walker.

Walker studied Holly's taut young

face, her wide shocked eyes, then looked at Jan.

"She can't possibly be that innocent!"

"Oh, but she is, incredible as it seems in this day and time," Jan mocked him. "Living with your grandmother in the depths of the jungle probably accounts for it. But don't worry about it. Connie and I will take care of her. And she'll outgrow it."

Walker looked back at Holly, who was watching him with the panic of a bird that suddenly spots a crouching cat.

"I would never have believed it," he said softly, and added quickly, "That leaves me nothing to say except good night."

At the door he turned to add, "If for any reason you need to get in touch with me, if there is anything I can do, you'll call me, won't you? I'm in the Manhattan phone book."

"Naturally," Jan mocked him. "But I'm quite sure Connie and I can handle everything. And don't be afraid we'll bother Mr. Beardsley."

Walker glanced back at Holly.

"Somehow I can't imagine any man being bothered if consulted about Holly," he admitted, and flashed Jan a grin that startled her because it was so attractively boyish and conspiratorial.

She listened to his footsteps going down the outside stairs. She turned to Holly who had dropped into a chair and put her face in her hands.

"It's getting late, honey, and tomorrow's a working day," Jan reminded her gently. "Better get some sleep so you can be all bright-eyed and full of zip come the dawn."

9

WHILE Jan had been doing her training as an airline stewardess, her mother had married again, with Jan's wholehearted approval, for she liked very much the kind, gentle man who had become her stepfather. His devotion to her mother, her mother's quiet, serene happiness, so different from the early years of Jan's childhood, had delighted her.

It was one of the few things she did not like about her job that she was able so seldom to see her mother, now living in Kansas with her small-town businessman husband. When she received a telephone call a few days after Holly moved in saying her mother was quite ill Jan packed and flew west immediately.

She was gone almost a month, until assured of her mother's eventual recovery. Because she was confident of the skill and competence of the surgeon and accepted without question that her mother would be all right now, Jan returned to her job. In New York she picked up her usual flight and returned to Palm Beach.

It was mid-afternoon when she came back to the apartment. She had not notified Connie or Holly of her return, so she planned a festive surprise dinner as a celebration of her homecoming.

She was in the small kitchenette, in toreador pants and a thin shirt, when she heard Connie and Holly on the stairs and came to the kitchenette doorway to greet them.

It was a gay and tumultuous greeting. Holly disappeared into her bedroom, leaving Connie and Jan to chatter as Jan finished dinner and set the table.

"Two places, pal, not three," said Connie as she took up the extra place. "Holly doesn't dine here any more."

Jan's eyebrows arched a bit.

"She and Hal must be getting along fine."

"Oh, she's not seeing Hal any more, or any of the other bright young men who hang out at the office," Connie answered dryly. "Brace yourself while I tell you, Jannie me dear; our Holly now goes around steady with Greg Channing."

Jan's mouth fell open and her eyes widened.

"Not *the* Greg Channing!" she gasped.

"I'd sure as blazes hate to think there was more than one of them! International, if slightly aging, playboy. So much money he has to hire people to help him count it, as wary of marriage as a shot-over bird-dog, yet every woman's dream-boat — that never drops anchor!"

"But, Connie, he must be fifty if he's a day!"

"Forty-one, it says in *Who's-Who-and-How-Come*," Connie answered.

Jan was astounded and incredulous.

"Then he can't possibly be interested in a child like Holly!"

"Oh, can't he? He positively drools over her."

"But, Connie, how could Holly possibly meet a man like Greg Channing? A shy, scared-to-death chick like Holly — " Jan broke off as Connie gave a raucous, mirthless laugh.

"Shy? Scared to death? Our Holly? Baby, you've been away too long."

"I've been gone a month."

"And a heap of things have happened, my friend," Connie assured her wearily. "Greg's a heavy investor in our firm; in fact, if it wasn't for his money I doubt if we'd be developing that Coral Shores sub-division. He came in to say 'how-do' to my boss. Seems his yacht had just dropped anchor in the harbor for the season and he was paying his respects. And it just happened that Holly brought some papers to my boss' desk while Greg was there — and it just happened that Greg took one look, pointed his neatly manicured finger and said, 'I'll have that, thanks a lot!' He's been wining and dining her ever since."

"But he can't possibly be serious!" Alarm was in Jan's face and in her voice.

"Of course not," Connie brushed that aside. "But *she* is, and that's what frightens me."

"We'll have to put a stop to it," said Jan firmly, and Connie eyed her curiously.

"Famous last words!" she mocked.

Holly came dancing into the room, and Jan's eyes widened as she stared at the costume Holly was wearing, an exquisite frock of ivory taffeta, embossed with small golden roses, and a scarf of golden-yellow lined with ivory slipped carelessly from one shoulder.

"Like it?" she demanded eagerly, and twirled before them.

"What, no mink?" mocked Connie dryly.

Holly laughed. "Oh, mink is so

common, don't you think? Greg says it is."

"Many a smart man has saved himself quite a piece of change by telling his gal-friend that — and getting her to believe it," Connie reminded her.

"Holly, where did you get that dress?" demanded Jan sternly.

Holly stared at her. "It's not really mine, Jan. I have to return it to Cecelie in the morning — provided I don't spill anything on it, and I'd better not, because the price tag on it said 'seven hundred dollars'!"

She looked from one to the other and nodded in agreement with the thought expressed in their eyes.

"Can you imagine anybody paying seven hundred dollars for just one dress?" she marvelled innocently.

"For that price, I'd expect half a dozen dresses, a suit, a fur coat — and first class passage to Italy," Connie agreed dryly.

"Look, fill me in, will you? Remember, I've been away!"

There was the sound of mellow music from outside — Jan could not believe that it was an automobile horn — but knew that it must be, for Holly caught up a small jeweled bag that matched the fabulous frock and hurried out, throwing over her shoulder a gay, "Tell her all about Greg, Connie. I mustn't keep him waiting."

The door banged shut behind her and the soft whisper of gold-shod feet on the stairs came back to them.

Connie was watching Jan, and there was a curious sardonic amusement in her eyes that did not quite conceal the anxiety there.

"Remember the day we picked her up on the beach and brought her here? And how sorry we were for her? Sounds pretty silly, doesn't it?"

"What did she mean about having to return that dress?"

"Oh, it seems that she owes the beautiful clothes as well as the exciting dates to our friend Greg."

"Connie! You can't mean she's

letting him buy her clothes?"

"Not buy them, no. Provide them, yes! Seems he has a pal who's opened up a smart and very, very exclusive shop here. I understand from Holly that Greg is financing the guy. The shop is small and ambitious. It's very important for the gowns to be seen, so Greg sees to it that Holly is seen in all the best places wearing Cecil's most inspired creations. The shop is called Cecelie's but the fellow's name is Cecil."

Connie paused, waited for all that to sink into Jan's stunned mind, and added dryly, "Nice going for our little 'girl outside' the best of everything, don't you think?"

"It's fantastic, incredible — "

"But the ghastly truth, pet, so you may as well face it," Connie told her. "And now let's eat. I'm starving."

Jan sat at the small table, but she had no interest in her food. As Connie ate, Jan said at last, "Connie, we've got to stop this business."

"Between Holly and Greg? How, if I may ask? She's almost nineteen, remember — and we're not her legal guardians."

"That's it — her legal guardians — "

"Poor Hubert? Jan, you're raving!"

"No, Hubert is not her legal guardian."

"*Mrs.* Hubert is? I'm sure she'd be glad to hold the girl's head under water until bubbles stopped coming up — but I can't imagine her showing any other interest in her."

"I suppose it will have to be Walker Lamont," Jan said reluctantly. "I'd rather take a licking than see him again. But something's got to be done, Connie!"

Connie put down her knife and fork and sighed.

"Jan, for Pete's sake, the kid is on her own. She's on Cloud Nine. 'Most any girl her age — and a lot of them a whole lot older — would give their eyeteeth to be in her spot!"

"But, Connie, don't you see? Greg

Channing will tire of her and drop her. And she'll have been spoiled for any other man who comes along — "

"That's our worry?" asked Connie grimly.

"Connie, you know it is!" Jan pleaded earnestly. "She's probably already in love with Channing. It will break her heart when he drops her. And he will! He's never been known to stick to one girl more than a few months at the most. And a girl like Holly, simple and unsophisticated and as out of place in his world as a brown wren in a bird of paradise preserve — I'm surprised he isn't already tired of her."

"You saw her when she left just now? Can you imagine even a Greg Channing getting tired of a girl who looks like that?"

"Yes, I can imagine his getting bored with her, the moment someone else with as much beauty and more sophistication came along," Jan insisted.

"Well, I suppose it could be that you're right, although I can't see what we can do about it," Connie answered, frankly weary of the whole subject. "I don't know just what you promised Beardsley and that Lamont fellow. All I thought we were expected to do was provide her with bed and board and a job by which she could pay for same. I didn't know we had made ourselves responsible for her immortal soul!"

"She's still working at the office?" Jan preferred to ignore the jibe.

"If you can call it working," Connie agreed. "She floats around with her head in the clouds, and the whole 'pool' hates her like sin, because somebody is always having to cover for her or redo her work. But the boss wouldn't dare fire her — not as long as she is Greg Channing's girl friend."

"That's — why, that's horrible, Connie! I tell you, it's got to stop!"

"Then suppose, Gran'ma Wilkes, you stop it! My head is bloody and definitely bowed from running into a stone wall," she said fiercely. "She may pay attention to you — she certainly won't to me. And what are you going to tell her? That Greg is too old for her? I did, and she gave me that wide-eyed innocent look and said sweetly, 'But I *like* older people. I've always been accustomed to them. Young people make me feel shy and awkward. I feel completely at home with Greg. He's wonderful'."

"The little fool!" Jan raged helplessly.

Connie looked down at her derisively.

"Oh, no, I think she's the smart one. You and I are the fools, to work as hard as we do," she mocked. "Sunday mornings, Greg calls for her in that Rolls and drives her to Cecelie's, where her costumes for the week are fitted. One is delivered to her every day, and yesterday's is picked up and returned to the shop. After the fittings Greg takes her to lunch on the yacht, and they run down to Miami, or just loaf along the inland waterway. He brings her back here in the late afternoon, she dons whatever Cecil wishes her to wear, and Greg takes her dining and dancing wherever Cecil's choice will get the best display! And you're going to try to stop all that?"

"But, Connie, you know it can't *last* — "

"Maybe not," Connie agreed. "But she's having herself a ball while it does, and she's young enough to have time to spare before she settles down to getting married to a man in what you call her own world. How do we know she won't meet some marriage-minded guy in Channing's sphere?"

"We don't, of course, but I don't think it's very likely, do you?"

"Likely? It's no more unlikely than her snagging Greg's attention and getting all this spread out before her! Stop it, if you can and if you feel you must, but frankly, I don't believe you can, and equally frankly, I don't see why you should feel the necessity."

And for a long moment the two eyed each other, farther apart in their thoughts than they had been in their years of friendship.

10

IN the past weeks since she had first met Greg, Holly had grown accustomed to the way he was greeted when they went out dining and dancing. No matter how many people were waiting for a table, one always appeared as if by magic for Greg. A maitre d' always escorted them to their table and hovered attentively, while Greg consulted with a waiter or two about the menu. When they rose to dance the orchestra leader always saluted Greg, and Holly felt blissful and excited to be his date.

Now and then in fleeting moments she would remember dates she had had with young men in the office, particularly Hal, a tall, thin, very earnest bespectacled young man whose evening's entertainment ran to a cafeteria dinner and a second-run movie at a double-feature house too far up Clematis Street.

Tonight, as she and Greg entered Valencia Gardens, the newest and most exclusive night spot on the Beach, a dance was ending. Guided by the maitre d', Holly and Greg were threading their way through the dancers returning to their tables when suddenly Holly stopped in front of a very good-looking young man.

"Oh, Mr. Lamont," she said eagerly, "how nice to see you. May I present Mr. Channing?"

Charles Lamont stared at her, while his dance partner paused, looking jealously at Holly. Greg scowling slightly, looked swiftly from Holly to Charles.

"Oh, hello, Uncle Greg," said Charles, laughing as he extended his hand. "How about introducing me to the lovely lady? I'm sure we've met, but where? Round Hill? Palm Springs?"

"Of course not, Mr. Lamont. It was at the Hacienda and at your sister's villa," Holly protested. "I'm Holly Tolliver."

"Oh, no!" gasped Charles, and his wide eyes swept over her, recalling with an effort the awkward, big-eyed, scared child he had seen on that occasion.

"Have I changed that much," asked Holly curiously, as impulsively as a child.

"Changed?" Charles' tone dismissed the word as shockingly inadequate. "You've blossomed, Holly, so much so that I wonder Caro would allow you inside the villa."

"Oh, I'm not at the villa any longer," Holly boasted happily. "I have an apartment and a job."

Charles managed *not* to look significantly at Greg, and to smile at Holly instead.

"Well, hooray for you, Holly," he answered, and nodded to Greg. "Nice to have seen you, Uncle Greg."

He followed his dinner date to a table, and Greg and Holly once more moved along behind the hovering maitre d' to their own table. When they were established and enormous menus had been placed in their hands, Holly glanced up at Greg, smiling.

"I didn't know you knew the Lamonts," she said eagerly.

Greg studied her for a moment, his eyes quite cold.

"And I didn't know you knew them — Chuck especially — and for a moment there I doubted that you did. I thought that was as brazen a piece of effrontery as I have ever witnessed, a deliberate 'pick-up' right in the middle of the dance-floor!" His tone was icy, and Holly blinked beneath it as though she stepped suddenly beneath a shower of ice-water.

"But, Greg, I told you about them — the Lamonts — how they found me at the Hacienda when Gran died — " she began, bewildered, puzzled by his manner.

"So you did!" Greg was still annoyed. "But since it's obvious that Chuck had quite forgotten you — "

"I'm sorry," said Holly meekly, frightened by his anger as much as she was puzzled by it.

Greg was consulting with the waiter about their dinner, and she clenched her hands tightly beneath the table's edge, waiting, watchful. She could not, of course, know that Greg's anger was not directed at herself half as much as at Chuck. 'Uncle Greg' indeed!

A little later, as they were dining, Chuck came to the table and said pleasantly, "Do you mind if Miss Tolliver dances with me, Uncle Greg?"

Holly caught her breath against the black rage that for a moment stood naked in Greg's eyes.

"I do, Chuck," said Greg grimly. "I mind very much. But I will consent on one condition — which is that you never again as long as you live call me 'Uncle Greg'."

Chuck laughed and held out his hand to Holly, who hesitated a moment before she accepted it and let him help her slip out from behind the table.

"Sorry, sir," Chuck assured Greg, and the 'sir' rasped Greg almost as much as the 'Uncle Greg' had done. "It's been a lifelong habit, but I'll try to curb it."

"I'd be very grateful," said Greg sharply.

As they moved out on the small dance floor and Chuck's arms went about her, he grinned down at Holly.

"What have you and Uncle — I mean Greg — been fighting about? He's in a towering rage, I know. I've known him since infancy practically, and I can always see when storm signals are flying."

"He thinks I tried to 'pick you up' — that I'd never really met you before."

Chuck nodded. "I can see how that would be, since I was such a fool I didn't recognize you at first."

"Well, after all, you *did* say I'd changed," she pointed out.

"Which is the understatement of the century, Beautiful." Chuck's arm

144

tightened slightly about her. "You must give me a chance to know you better. How about dinner tomorrow night with me?"

"I'm sorry, but I'm all tied up," said Holly.

She did not quite grasp the change that came into his eyes, but his arms loosened a bit about her and his tone was dry.

"Of course it's with Greg," he answered.

"Four nights a week I dine with him and go dancing, so people can see Cecelie's clothes," she told him simply.

Puzzled, Chuck said, "Now there, I'm afraid, you lost me. Who's Cecelie?"

"The dress designer. Greg is backing him and it's very important that his gowns be seen in all the right places."

"But I could take you to the right places, Holly, on your free nights."

"I don't have any free nights," Holly told him. "The nights I'm not showing Cecelie's clothes I go to school."

"Oh, so you're a model."

Holly laughed. "Oh, no, I'm a clerk-typist in Hibart-Jordan's real estate office," she answered. "I go to night school."

"To learn to be a better clerk-typist?"

She shook her head. "To learn poise and self-confidence and dancing."

When he still looked puzzled, she added, "It's a charm school."

Chuck held her a little away from him and stared down at her, his brows drawn together in a scowl.

"I've heard about gilding the lily, but this is ridiculous," he assured her firmly. "*You* going to charm school."

"Oh, but it isn't," she insisted earnestly. "Remember what I was like when you first met me?"

"Er — vaguely."

"And how, tonight, you said I'd 'blossomed'?"

"I do, indeed, and so you have. And to a dazzling degree."

"That's the charm school," she

told him. "I took a lot of gilding, Mr. Lamont."

"Hey, wait a minute," Chuck protested. "My brother Walker is Mr. Lamont. Me, I'm Chuck, the black sheep of the family."

"I don't believe that," Holly protested earnestly, "that you're a black sheep — or that you could be."

Chuck's eyebrows went up a little.

"Hey, they did a good job on you at the charm school, didn't they?" he mocked.

"I hope so. I was so sick of always being the girl outside — outside of all the fun and good times and pretty clothes and dates."

"Well, being all tied up four nights a week with Greg and two nights a week at the charm school — by the way, what do you do with your day off? It's the law, you know, that you must have one!"

"Oh, on my day off, I have my hair and nails done, and fit the frocks I'm going to wear the next week, and usually Greg and I go for a cruise on his yacht. We went to Miami last week, to the races. I'd never seen a horse race before, and I loved it!"

"It sounds like quite a busy schedule," Chuck agreed, and once again there was an odd, speculative look in his eyes that she could not quite understand. "So now you have an apartment and a job."

11

GREG was watching Chuck and Holly floating about the small, cramped dance floor when a tall, regal-looking blonde stopped beside his table and said throatily, "Good evening, Greg. Incredible to believe I'd ever see you alone in a place like this."

Greg stood up, his handsome face taut, his eyes cold.

"Good evening, Evelyn. Nice to see you again." His tone was as cold as his eyes and his hands clenched as she slid, uninvited, into Holly's seat and smiled across at him.

"Of course I saw you when you came in with that delightful-looking child," cooed Evelyn sweetly. "What happened to her? Did you send her back to the nursery for bread and milk?"

"She's dancing with Chuck Lamont,"

Greg told her harshly.

"Oh, I see them now. A very handsome couple they make, don't they?" Evelyn's voice was warm honey. "Really, Greg, I'm surprised to see you cradle-snatching. You aren't old enough for that — yet."

Greg had his temper under control now, and though it was a smile that had little mirth, he managed to smile at her.

"It couldn't possibly be that you're just a mite jealous, darling?" he asked pleasantly.

A dark, ugly color crept up beneath Evelyn's delicate make-up, and her blue eyes hardened.

"Naturally I'm jealous of every woman you look at, and a devil of a lot of good it does me," she answered evenly, her voice husky. "But when I see you out with a mere child like that, it doesn't make me jealous; it just disgusts me."

For a moment he had difficulty controlling his fury, but he would not give her the satisfaction of knowing that she had hit home.

"I'm sorry you feel that way, Evelyn." His voice was dry despite the smoldering fury in his dark eyes. "She's really a lovely girl, and I enjoy being with her."

"You mean you enjoy being seen with her because she is so lovely all the other men envy you," she cut in swiftly. "But it hurts me, Greg, to see you dating a mere child."

"Now, why should anything I do hurt you, my pet?" In his tone the phrase was an insult, cold, deliberate, stinging, deepening her color as though the blow had been physical rather than verbal.

"You know the answer to that, Greg. Because I love you, of course," she told him, and raised a silencing hand as he would have answered roughly. "Oh, I know you never loved me, or even pretended to. You just let me make a fool of myself, until finally I couldn't take it any longer."

"And ran off and married someone else."

"Because I knew you'd never marry me."

"I never said I would."

"I know. But I thought maybe I could make myself so important to you that — " she shrugged and managed a thin-lipped smile, her eyes bitter and deeply hurt. "Of course, I couldn't be wise enough to know that nobody in the world is really important to you, except yourself. The whole world has to be geared to your demands."

"Much more of this, Evelyn, and you'll be weeping hysterically and disgracing yourself. I know you so well. These tirades invariably end in tears."

Her eyes were bright and hot and dry, like the faint smile that touched her faintly tremulous mouth.

"Oh, not any more, Greg! You'll be happy to know I got over all that silliness quite a while ago. I don't think I have any more tears to shed."

152

"Well, that's a relief," said Greg brutally.

Chuck and Holly were coming toward them now, and Greg stood up to greet them. Evelyn stayed where she was, studying Holly with a coldly analytical gaze as the girl paused at the table and smiled at her.

"Mrs. Stanley, Miss Tolliver," Greg made the introductions he could not avoid. "And you probably know Charles Lamont, Evelyn."

"Of course, Mrs. Stanley," Chuck greeted her pleasantly. "How's Bill?"

Evelyn's eyebrows knit in a slightly puzzled frown.

"Bill?" she repeated as though she had never heard the name before.

Chuck colored and glanced swiftly at Greg, who was regarding him with cool, amused disdain.

"Why, I meant Bill Stanley, of course — your husband."

"Oh, *that* Bill!" Evelyn laughed lightly as she stood up. "I haven't seen him in ages. We've been divorced for two years. I did hear that he'd gone on safari to Africa. With the Mau-Maus, the political experts and all the bored rich Americans safari-ing all over Africa, I should think it would be terribly crowded, wouldn't you?"

Chuck glanced helplessly at Greg, who merely smiled and refused to come to his rescue.

Evelyn studied Holly for a moment, smiling with her lips only, and drawled, "What a lovely frock, Miss Tolliver."

"Oh, do you like it? I'm so glad." Holly beamed innocently at her. "It's a Cecelie original."

Evelyn said pleasantly, "Cecelie? I don't think I know her."

"It's in the Via Parigi, a small new shop, and they have lovely things," Holly told her eagerly.

Evelyn laughed, flung a glance at Greg and drawled, "I must look in on Cecelie. Nice to have seen you, Greg, Chuck — and delightful to have met you, Miss Tolliver."

She walked away, and Chuck glanced

uneasily at Greg's taut face and then at Holly, who was smiling innocently at him.

"Thanks for the dance, Holly — and good night, Greg," said Chuck and, with his back very straight, walked back to his own table.

Greg made no effort to help Holly slip back into the seat Evelyn had vacated, and his tone was curt as he said, "Shall we go?"

Holly looked at him swiftly and then down at the table.

"But we haven't finished our dinner," she began.

"It's ruined now and quite inedible," Greg insisted, put his hand beneath her elbow and guided her firmly toward the exit.

Outside in the silver-lit fragrance of the moon-drenched night while they waited for the attendant to bring his car around, he growled at her half under his breath, "I must have Cecil arrange a couple of signboards for you to wear, sandwich-man fashion, giving his name and address. And perhaps we should put the price tags back on the gowns."

Holly protested, bewildered, "But Mrs. Stanley liked the dress. I only wanted her to know it was from Cecelie's."

The car slid to a halt in front of them, and Greg bundled her into it unceremoniously and slipped beneath the wheel.

"I'm sorry if I did anything that annoyed you," she stammered miserably.

"Leaving me to sit at the table alone while you cavorted with that Lamont creature." He bit off the angry words as he shot the car at a dangerous pace along Brazilian Way and into the Trail.

"But you said you didn't mind my dancing with him if he'd stop calling you Uncle Greg — and he did!"

"I don't care to discuss it," Greg told her shortly. He brought the car to an abrupt halt in front of the garage-apartment and waited for her to alight. Usually he got out, swung the door open for her, and walked with her along the drive to the steps leading up to the apartment. Tonight he merely waited with barely concealed impatience for her to get herself out of his way so he could drive off.

She stood for a moment beside the car, a slender exquisitely lovely ghost in her white frock against the dark shrubbery, and asked humbly, "Will I see you tomorrow?"

Greg flung her a glance that she could not decipher.

"At the moment I don't know," he told her coldly. "I may be going out of town for a while. I'll give you a ring at the office tomorrow when my plans are completed."

And with a spurt of gravel, the car shot backward into the street and was gone, leaving Holly to stare after it, wideeyed, deeply hurt and even more deeply puzzled.

12

LATE in the afternoon of her next New York day off, Jan walked down Fifty-Second Street, her heart beating at an unpleasantly accelerated speed. Walker Lamont had been civil, quite pleasant when she had finally managed to get him on the phone. He had seemed amused and only slightly curious when she had asked to see him and had blurted out that it had to do with Holly. He had suggested this cocktail lounge near his office and she had breathed a sigh of relief. She hadn't wanted to go to his office and she had very much wanted to talk to him privately.

Remembering the last time they had talked, she felt color pour into her face and writhed with humiliation that she must turn to him, after she had been so contemptuously sure that she never would. But she couldn't just stand idly by and watch Holly heading straight for heartbreak and disaster.

She had dressed very carefully, and she knew she was looking very well in her new tweed suit with the matching topcoat about her shoulders, and the trim new hat was vastly becoming. She'd worried a little about that when she had bought it this afternoon. Was it too becoming to be fashionable?

Walker was waiting when she entered the tiny foyer, and his eyes swept her appreciatively, without the slightest trace of recognition, and looked beyond her.

"I'm sorry if I'm late, Mr. Lamont." She stood beside him, and Walker looked down at her, startled.

"Miss Wilkes?" he asked uncertainly. Jan laughed, remembering that the only time he had ever seen her she had been wearing toreador pants and a shirt and her hair had been disheveled.

"I'm Jan Wilkes, Mr. Lamont. Thanks for not recognizing me," she mocked lightly. "It restores my confidence."

"I can't imagine your confidence needing to be restored," Walker assured her, and looked quite pleased as he walked beside her into the crowded lounge where quite a few people greeted him and eyed Jan with friendly admiration and curiosity.

Seated, a waiter beside them, Walker raised his eyebrows questioningly at Jan, who said quickly, "A martini will be fine."

The waiter moved away, and Jan faced Walker.

"I suppose it must seem very odd to you, Mr. Lamont, my telephoning you."

"Not odd. Let's say unexpected — and very pleasant. I'd been hoping you would, one of these days," Walker answered courteously, his eyes warmly admiring.

"It's about Holly."

"So I gathered from what you said on the telephone. What's she up to now?"

Jan hesitated and then asked, "Do you know a Gregory Channing, Mr. Lamont?"

"Of course — doesn't everybody?" Walker grinned and added, "The name is Walker, Janet."

"Thanks — and my friends call me Jan."

"Good! Now that we've got that out of the way, what's Gregory Channing got to do with Holly?"

The drinks came, and as she sipped hers Jan told him as briefly as she could what she had discovered on her return from visiting her mother. Walker listened without comment, his brows drawing together as the story unfolded. When it was finished, he studied her curiously.

"Our little gal from the Hacienda seems to have turned into a real glamour gal, if she can keep Greg Channing interested this long!" he commented at last. "That takes a bit of doing. I don't remember her very well; I only saw her twice. But she's surely the last person in the world I'd ever expect to fascinate Greg. Still — she seemed to have quite an effect on my brother-in-law. I can't quite understand, Jan, what you expect me to do about it."

Jan turned the cocktail glass around in her fingers, not quite willing to meet his eyes for fear of what he might see in her own. And Walker waited, watching her, liking what he saw: the smartly dressed copper-colored hair with the small dab of a hat setting off its shimmering waves, the smoky-gray tweed suit with its immaculate white blouse, the soft curve of her cheek, the rose-red of her lovely mouth.

"I know it's silly of me to ask you to help me rescue her." Jan looked up at him, and he saw that her eyes were green and that there was a faint shimmer of tears misting them. "It's just that she's so very young, so vulnerable, so helpless!"

"Like a stray kitten?"

Startled, Jan said, "Imagine you

remembering that."

"It painted a picture that gave me quite a clear view of you, what you're really like when you aren't trading insults," Walker told her, and grinned as the color poured into her face.

"It was unforgivable of me, the way I talked to you — "

"It wasn't, at all," Walker assured her. "Under the circumstances as you knew them it was quite understandable. I didn't know the girl at all, I had only what my sister had told me to go on, and my sister was outraged, jealous."

"But she had no reason to be, honestly! Mr. Beardsley looked on Holly with an almost fatherly interest."

"How do you know that's not the same way Channing looks on her?"

"Oh, don't be ridiculous!" Jan snapped hotly.

Walker laughed. "Very soon now, at this rate, we'll be back at the hurled insults stage," he reminded her.

"I'm sorry," she said miserably. "But, you see, Holly imagines herself madly in love with Greg Channing. You and I both know that the last thing in the world in Channing's mind is marriage to *any* woman — least of all a girl like Holly. So what can we do to keep her from being hurt when he drops her, as we both know he will?"

"Thanks," said Walker quietly.

Bewildered, Jan studied him.

"Thanks for what?"

"For including me in your plans. You did say 'we,' didn't you?"

"Well, yes, of course. Why else would I have come to you like this?"

"Of course," said Walker. "I'm very grateful that you did, but I have to admit that I can't see anything that either or both of us can do. Holly's of age, I have no legal claim of guardianship that I might call on her to make her obey any orders I gave even if she *would* listen to a legal guardian or anyone else."

Jan hesitated for a long moment and at last forced herself to ask humbly, "You don't think maybe if you had a talk with Channing — "

Walker stared at her, dumbfounded. "My dear girl!" he protested. "What are you trying to do — needle me into getting a poke in the nose from Channing? Because that's all that would happen. He'd tell me to mind my own blankety-blank business — and so he should. If Holly were, say, my sister, or even my legal ward — even then I'd hesitate, because that kind of opposition only fouls things up still more."

"It was a silly idea," Jan agreed, subdued. "I thought of going to him, but I have no authority over her either, and I'm sure he'd order me out of the house, as he'd have every right to do."

"Oh, I don't think he'd be that rough on a lovely gal like you," Walker tried to comfort her. "That's always been his weak point — lovely ladies." He broke off, alarmed, as she looked up at him, her eyes widening. "Hey, now, get that look out of your eyes! You're *not* going to Channing and try to take him away from Holly — and then laugh in his face."

Jan's eyes were enormous as she listened, and then cut in, "Well, for goodness sake, I never meant to go near the man! But now that you suggest it — "

"I did *not* suggest it! I saw the idea forming in your mind — and you get it right out of there immediately," Walker ordered sternly. "He's not your kind at all. Oh, he's handsome and charming and the ladies swoon over him. But you're much too decent and honest and straightforward to waste so much as a thought on the man! I won't have it, do you understand?"

Jan's head was up now, and her green eyes were cold.

"Please keep your voice down, Mr. Lamont," she said through her teeth. "And I'm afraid you have even less authority over me than you do over Holly."

For a moment they glared at each other furiously. Then, to Jan's angry amazement, Walker laughed, although the laugh did not quite wipe out the anger in his eyes.

"What's so funny?" Jan demanded icily.

"We are — you and I both," Walker told her. "I knew if we sat here long enough we'd reach the place where we started brawling. I've only met you twice, but each time the meeting ended in a brawl."

"You can be so exasperating."

"And so can you," Walker reminded her. "And what do you say that we bury the hatchet, though not in each other's scalp and try to figure out some way to rescue Holly from her unfortunate attachment? That is, if she *wants* to be rescued. Does she?"

"Of course not! She's mad about the man! They quarreled because your brother Charles danced with her a few nights ago, and she was all broken up until Channing telephoned and made up. Now she's worse than ever."

"Oh, so Chuck has met her and

danced with her," Walker drawled thoughtfully. "I wonder what he thought of her."

"He asked her for a date, she said, but she turned him down! 'Greg darling' keeps her too busy to date other men."

Walker looked at her with sudden enthusiasm.

"Now, why wouldn't something like that be wise? Expose her to young men who possess good looks, charm — "

Jan shook her head. "She doesn't like young men, they bore her, she's lived all her life with older people."

"She sounds like a gal who missed out on some badly needed spankings not too long ago," he said grimly.

Jan reached for her bag and gloves, preparatory to saying goodbye.

"I'm so sorry to have bothered you, Walker," she told him. "But I mustn't keep you any longer. I'm sure you have plans for the evening."

Walker reached for the bag and gloves, laid them back on the settee and said firmly, "I do indeed have plans for the evening, and they revolve right around you."

"Oh, but — "

"After all, we haven't decided what to do about Holly, have we?"

Jan shook her head, smiling faintly.

"All we've decided is that there's nothing we can do except stand by and pick up the pieces after it's all over and help her put them together again."

Walker studied her intently, and, Jan's green eyes widened and her color deepened beneath the warmth in his eyes.

13

CHUCK grinned pleasantly at the houseman who welcomed him and took his bags. He went up the steps and into the villa as Caro, smartly dressed for an afternoon party, came down the stairs.

"Why, Chuck, what are you doing here?" she demanded.

Deeply hurt, though there was a twinkle in his eyes, Chuck asked, "Now is that a warm-hearted welcome for a brother from his only sister?"

"Chuck, don't be an idiot," Caro protested. "What *are* you doing here?"

"Sampling the fleshpots and begging room and board for the weekend. And where else would I beg it but from my only sister?" Chuck asked. "You *do* have a spare room, don't you? The linen closet will do, and you can have one of the servants fling me a crust and a glass of water."

"You know Hubert and I are always glad to have you, Chuck, and there's always plenty of room for an extra guest," Caro assured him briskly. "I'm afraid you'll have to entertain yourself until dinner time. I'm late for a tea, and since I'm pouring, I'll have to rush. Hubert is probably at the cabaña. He spends most of his time on the beach these days, though I can't think what he can possibly find to do there. Read, I suppose. He's usually got his nose in a book."

She leaned toward Chuck, kissed the air a few inches from his cheek, mindful of her make-up, and hurried out to her waiting car.

Chuck grinned as he watched her and then turned to follow the houseman up to the room usually assigned to him on his infrequent visits. He dismissed the man, changed into slacks and a sports shirt and went down to the beach.

Hubert, lying relaxed in a long chair on the cabaña terrace, looked up,

171

scowling slightly as he saw Chuck approaching. And then as he recognized him, he stood up and greeted him with the cool hospitality he felt the occasion required.

"Nice to see you, Chuck," he said as they shook hands. "What brings you down?"

Chuck grinned wryly. "Oh, just a whim," he laughed. "Matter of fact, I've been visiting the Offermans and thought I'd drop in on you and Caro before going back to Canaveral."

"I'm afraid you won't see much of Caro. She's pretty busy. It seems to be quite a season."

Chuck accepted the drink Wilkins offered and dropped into a chair.

"I caught a glimpse of her as she was rushing off to a tea party," Chuck answered. "She's looking very handsome."

"Doesn't she always?" Hubert agreed pleasantly.

The talk between the two men was desultory, as was to be expected between two men who, though they were brothers-in-law, had so little in common and saw each other so seldom that they were practically strangers.

Chuck made somewhat heavy going of the conversation, and at last Hubert put down his half-finished drink and said quietly, "What's on your mind, Chuck?"

Chuck looked up at him and managed a grin that made him look much younger than his actual age.

"Why, nothing, really, Hubert."

"You may go, Wilkins," said Hubert quietly, and Wilkins bowed and departed.

When he was out of earshot, Hubert said curtly, "Out with it, Chuck. What are you doing here?"

"Why, I just dropped in — " Chuck began defensively, and stopped as Hubert shook his head, smiling very slightly.

"Stow it, Chuck," he ordered. "You've 'just dropped in' not more than half a dozen times since Caro and I were married, and always it was when you were in some sort of jam. What is it this time?"

"I resent that! Can't a man visit his sister — "

"Resent and be damned! I know how you and Caro feel toward each other; you can't be in the same room five minutes without fighting like the cats of Kilkenny!" Hubert interrupted. "So come clean. If it's a jam I can help you out of, I'll do it, of course, as I always have. But don't let's have a lot of hypocrisy about your deep affection for your beloved sister. That, Chuck, won't wash. I know you both much too well to believe you came here because you wanted to see her."

Chuck looked down at his half-finished drink, turning the glass round and round between his hands, as he sought for words with which to clothe his thoughts. Hubert watched him, faint hostility in his eyes.

Chuck looked up at him suddenly, grave-eyed, and Hubert recognized an echo of his own hostility in Chuck's dark, cool eyes.

"What ever happened to that girl from the Hacienda?" Chuck asked.

The unexpectedness of this sharpened Hubert's hostility.

"Do you mean Holly Tolliver?" he asked.

"Of course. The girl who had lived with Gran all her life and we didn't know what to do with when we sold the Hacienda," Chuck explained. His tone was cool, faintly touched with derision, because they both knew exactly the girl he meant. "Caro brought her here to stay until Walker could figure out some sort of future for her. Where is she now?"

"Aren't you a bit tardy in displaying an interest in Holly?"

"Perhaps."

"Well, she's not here any more. She figured out a future for herself and saved you Lamonts the bother."

"And just what sort of future did she figure out?"

175

Hubert sat erect, scowling.

"She got herself a job as a clerk-typist and moved into a garage-apartment with two other girls," he said sharply.

"Nice girls, I hope? Respectable?"

"Do you think I'd have let her move in with them if they hadn't been?"

"Oh, you investigated them?"

"Certainly I investigated. See here, Chuck, I find all this very offensive," snapped Hubert sharply. "You and your brother dumped the girl on Caro as though she had been some inanimate bit of furniture. And now that she's found herself a job and a place to live and, I hope, some pleasant friends — "

"Oh, she's found some pleasant friends, all right! Right out of the top drawer. I imagine even Caro would be somewhat impressed by one of them, anyway."

Hubert glared at him, and before he could speak Chuck went on, "I understand Caro was very relieved when Holly moved out."

"What the devil are you getting at?"

"I saw Holly one night and didn't even recognize her, she's changed so much!" Chuck said quietly. "A real twenty-two-carat glamour girl. A raging beauty, no less."

Despite his angry bewilderment, Hubert made a little gesture of deprecation.

"Oh, come now, Chuck — you couldn't have seen Holly. She's not a glamour girl by any stretch of the imagination. A nice, shy, perhaps even pretty little girl — "

"Greg Channing thinks she's a knockout, and he ought to know," Chuck stated quietly.

Hubert swore under his breath, his eyes wide.

"Greg Channing?" he repeated incredulously. "You mean *he* knows Holly?"

"I think the classic phrase is: 'And how!'" Chuck answered grimly. "From what she told me when we were dancing, Greg is responsible for the glamour treatment: charm school, fancy duds, being seen in all the right places with Greg. I understand he doesn't allow her time to date anyone else. Seems to have a monopoly on her time, as it were!"

"Why, that's outrageous. Greg Channing is twice her age, and smooth as whipped butter. Holly's no match for him."

"I agree. So what are we going to do about it?"

Hubert stared at him as though he hadn't the faintest idea what Chuck was talking about.

"Do about it?" he repeated.

Chuck nodded, his young face taut and grave, his eyes meeting Hubert's squarely.

"Holly's a kid, much too nice a kid to be allowed to make a fool of herself about a man like Greg Channing," he stated flatly.

Hubert had himself under control now, though anger still blazed in his eyes.

"It strikes me, Chuck my boy, that

all this concern you're expressing for the girl is a bit overdue and even ludicrous," he said harshly. "You dumped her here on Caro and went away without showing the faintest interest in her. It wasn't until you saw that she had turned into a beauty that you became all hot and bothered about 'protecting' her."

"I know." Chuck nodded. "I suppose Walker and I thought vaguely Caro would look after her, see to it she had the right clothes, the right training — a decent chance at a decent life — "

"You really don't know Caro at all, do you?" Hubert mocked him grimly. "It never occurred to any of the three of you that when you sold the Hacienda and divided the check, Holly, by all rights, should have had that money? That would have given her what you call a decent chance, don't you think?"

"I guess we didn't think of it," Chuck admitted, chagrined.

"But now, when you see what she has become — "

"That's just it, Hubert. What *has* she become?"

Scowling, Hubert snapped, "What the devil do you mean by that?"

"Being monopolized by Greg Channing — a girl outside his world, young, radiantly beautiful — " Chuck broke off and grinned wryly. "Go ahead and remind me that it's mostly the fault of the Lamonts that she's where she is now. But I want to know what can be done to spare her the inevitable heart break when he drops her, as, of course, he will."

"I'm afraid you'll have to go to somebody a darned sight wiser about women than I am for the answer to that, Chuck my lad!" Hubert drawled. "I'm hardly in a position to advise you, I'm afraid, even if I wanted to, and I'm not at all sure that I do."

Chuck's eyes met his straightly.

"You are not even mildly concerned about what happens to the girl?" he asked gravely.

"And why should I be? She's a Lamont responsibility, remember. I helped her get away from here and into an apartment with a couple of thoroughly respectable girls of whom she seemed quite fond. I'm afraid I consider my responsibility ended right there," Hubert spelled it out for him firmly.

Chuck nodded. "I suppose Caro was pretty jealous of her."

"Don't be a fool! Caro scarcely knew the girl was in the house."

Chuck stood up, grinned without mirth and nodded.

"That buttons it up, then," he said quietly. "Looks as if I must be the one to rescue our little gal from the big, bad wolf."

"Greg Channing is a very attractive man, Chuck. What makes you so sure she *wants* to be rescued?" Hubert demanded.

Chuck considered that for a thoughtful moment, and then he nodded.

"There's that, of course," he admitted.

"But I think I'll have a try at it, anyway."

He nodded to Hubert, turned and strode back toward the beach stairs while Hubert watched him, angry, yet amused, too. So little Holly, the small, frightened mouse, had crept out of her hole in the servants' wing and turned into a fairy princess, with Prince Charming played by Greg Channing!

That evening while Caro was dressing for dinner, Hubert knocked punctiliously at the door of her dressing room and came in. His dark silk robe was belted tightly about his waist, his hands were jammed into his pockets and there was a look of amusement in his eyes.

Caro, bending close to the well-lit mirror, drawing a lipstick brush with meticulous care across her thin lips, glanced up at him without quite daring to smile until her job was finished. And then, carefully examining the lush mouth she had drawn for herself, she glanced up at him, smiling.

"You're not dressed, darling," she cooed.

"Oh, there's plenty of time," he assured her. "I just had a thought, Caro — someone I'd like you to ask to dinner as soon as you can manage it."

"Of course, darling! Who?"

"Gregory Channing."

Caro blinked. "But for goodness sake, Hubert, why Greg Channing?"

"Oh, there's a little business deal — nothing vastly important, of course, but I just thought if he had been a guest in our house, it might make things a bit easier. I've met him around, but I've never had a chance to get to know him." Hubert was quite casual.

"Well, if you think he'd come," Caro answered. "I'd love to have him, naturally — what hostess wouldn't? But he's pretty elusive. I think he plays around with a more informal crowd."

She moved to her desk, and opened her engagement book, running her eye down the list.

"How about Thursday night?" she suggested, intent on the book.

"Fine."

"Now, let's see, whom shall I ask for his dinner partner?" Caro puzzled.

"Why not let him choose his own?"

Caro looked up, puzzled.

"But really, darling, that's dangerous, don't you think? Greg's taste in women friends is a bit free-wheeling. He might bring somebody who wouldn't be acceptable to our friends."

"Oh, I think you can safely trust him this year," Hubert answered, and the twinkle in his eyes disturbed Caro.

"Well, of course, if you feel it would be safe." Caro frowned down at the engagement book. "I really don't know anyone down here this season who is likely to be a chosen pal of Greg Channing's. His crowd is the café society kind, and I don't know anything about them."

She preened herself unconsciously as she said it, and Hubert watched her, amused yet somehow touched.

She was so proud of her social position, her prestige, and guarded it so jealously. Which, he told himself, might be one reason her parties, so beautifully managed, were sometimes so painfully dull.

"Thanks for asking him, dear," he said politely.

"Oh, I'm so glad you wanted me to," Caro told him earnestly. "I'm always so happy when you show an interest in my parties, when you want me to invite friends of yours."

"You're very sweet, my dear. I'm sorry I'm such a boor."

Caro clung to him for a moment, forgetful of her make-up, forgetful of everything except this rare moment of tenderness between them.

"You're not, darling. You're everything any sane woman could want in a husband," she assured him with a warmth he somehow found oddly embarrassing.

14

THE Hibiscus Club was located at the northern end of the island. It was one of the resort's favorite night spots, and its opening night of the season was always a social event. Tonight it was jammed.

As Holly, in one of Cecelie's most inspired gowns and escorted by Greg, entered the foyer, Chuck grinned at her warmly.

"Hello, Holly, you're looking exquisite," he greeted her.

Color touched Holly's face and her eyes were eager.

"Oh, Chuck, nice to see you. Thanks!"

Greg nodded curtly at Chuck and said coldly, "Good evening, Charles. Without a reservation?"

"I'm afraid so," Chuck admitted ruefully. "I wasn't sure I was going to be in town. I don't suppose you could squeeze in a couple of more chairs at your table?"

"That's quite impossible. It's a table for two," Greg assured him firmly, and marched Holly past him and to the velvet rope that dropped before them.

At their table, Holly smiled at Greg and looked about the room.

"It's a lovely place, isn't it?" she said happily.

"Not too bad," Greg agreed, and accepted the menu placed before him by a solicitous waiter.

Holly ignored hers and as always waited for Greg to order for both of them, while she sat contentedly and looked about the room. The beautifully dressed women weren't a bit more glamorous, she told herself happily, than she was. Greg had assured her her frock was a success, and that, for Greg, constituted a compliment of no mean proportions.

When the waiter had gone, Greg looked across at Holly and smiled.

"That's a very nice little frock and you look charming in it," he told her lazily. "But we must see that Cecelie does even better than that for Thursday night."

Holly looked across the small table at him, bright-eyed.

"Oh? What's Thursday night?" she asked eagerly.

"We have a dinner invitation that both pleases and amuses me," he told her. "I'd have turned it down without a qualm except that it includes you and I'm very anxious to show you off, especially to these people."

"I hope I won't disgrace you," Holly said lightly.

His eyes chilled and his jaw set.

"You'd better not," he told her ominously.

For a moment she thought he was merely being amusing, and then she saw that there was no flippancy in his eyes.

"This is something I've been looking forward to for — oh, ever since we first met," he went on in that cold, ominous tone. "I want very much to show them what I've been able to do with you and *to* you. Otherwise I'd refuse to allow myself to be bored by going there. Because Caro Beardsley is the world's most crashing bore, and her parties are notorious for dullness. I accepted the invitation when she suggested I choose my own dinner companion."

Holly was staring at him, wide-eyed.

"We're going to dinner at the Beardsleys'?" she gasped.

"I think it should be quite amusing, don't you?"

"No! I don't think it would be amusing, and I don't want to go!"

Now there was no doubt of his chilling anger.

"You'll go, because I am determined to show you off."

"Why, she'd turn me out of the house."

"Oh, no, she wouldn't. She wouldn't dare, if you're with me, as you will be."

Holly stared at him and cringed before the look in his eyes.

"But why should you want to show me off to them? I've told you about when I lived there — "

"Which is one of the reasons you must go back with me, looking like a princess. And I shall expect you to 'snoot' the Beardsley woman with all the insolence you can manage. And it had better be quite a lot or I shall be very displeased with you."

All the warm friendliness, the gratitude, even the love she had felt for him seeped out of her like wine from a smashed glass. Meeting his cold, stern eyes, she felt as though a cold wind had suddenly blown over her bare shoulders, and she shivered in it.

"Do you understand?" he demanded. When she did not answer, because she could not trust her voice, he went on swiftly, "Every artist yearns to exhibit his creation, just as I want to exhibit you, because you are the girl I've created."

Holly drew a long breath, her hands tightly clenched beneath the table's edge.

"That's all I mean to you, isn't it?" she asked faintly.

Greg scowled at her. "Well, what else could you mean? If I merely wanted to be seen about with a lovely girl, beautifully dressed and with a certain sophistication, I can assure you I'd have no trouble finding half a dozen in my own crowd. But you presented a challenge that first day when I saw you in the realty office. And when you had dinner with me and I studied you, I saw all you needed was polishing and a setting and you could be quite devastating. You are now, and I want to flaunt you before the Beardsley woman and let her gnash her teeth."

"You aren't a bit in love with me, are you? asked Holly huskily.

His brows went up and there was a touch of derision in his eyes.

"My dear girl! I never for a moment indicated that I was."

"No, I know you didn't," Holly answered softly. "Which just makes it that much funnier that almost from the first I've been in love with you."

Greg brushed that aside as of no importance.

"I suppose so," he agreed carelessly. Obviously, it was no more than he had expected. In fact, he would have been disappointed if it hadn't happened. "But you must admit, Holly, that I've never even kissed you!"

"I know." Holly nodded, and her voice was no more than a breath. "I've wondered about that. There have been times when I ached to have you take me in your arms and kiss me."

"Then you were a very silly girl," Greg told her shortly. "I have no intention of getting myself involved in anything so silly as a love affair with a girl I've created myself."

Holly's wide, shocked eyes silenced him.

"So that was why you were so nice to me. You were like that man in *My Fair*

Lady who wanted to change a nobody into a somebody."

"Well, something like that," Greg seemed pleased by the comparison. "And I pride myself I've done a good job. But until you are exposed to people such as the Beardsleys entertain, I can't be quite sure that my work is finished. I think you can hold your own with that crowd, but I have to be sure. So we'll see on Thursday night."

"No!" Holly's voice rose a little.

Cold fury flashed in Greg's eyes.

"Keep your voice down, Holly. If you make a scene here — " he threatened.

"I won't make a scene if you'll take me home."

"That I most certainly will not do."

She started to rise, and his hand shot out and clamped with brutal force about her wrist, making her wince a little with pain.

"Chuck is outside," she stammered. "He'll take me."

"Don't be a fool. Chuck is with a

193

party. He can't leave them without them knowing you walked out on me. And that I will not allow."

"I'm going home."

"Walking all the way? That I doubt." The waiter came, serving the first course of the carefully chosen dinner, and Greg had to release her wrist. She slid as far away from him as the confines of the banquette would permit, well out of his reach, and Greg's eyes flashed a warning at her.

When the waiter had gone, Greg leaned toward her across the table, and the look in his eyes was like a physical blow.

"See here, Holly, I'm a fairly well known personality down here, as well as in New York." His words were small icicles that stung her flushed face. "No doubt there are newspaper columnists here, local, if not from the New York papers. If you walk out of here now, there'll be scandal."

"That shouldn't be such a novelty to you," Holly flung at him with far more spirit than he had expected.

"I don't know what's gotten into you, Holly," he growled at her, obviously surprised. "After all I've done for you — "

"Oh, please!" Holly lifted a shaking hand in protest. "Let's not have that routine. You've been very kind in your own way, though I can't see why. I thought it was because you were in love with me and wanted me to be a wife you could be proud of."

"You didn't expect me to marry you?" he protested.

"I didn't expect it, no." she confessed. "I just hoped for it."

"Well, that's your hard luck, my girl! I did nothing that would lead you to expect any such thing, and it was the last thing I ever expected," he told her with a restrained violence that darkened his angry face with color.

Moving so swiftly, so unexpectedly that he could not guess her intention fast enough to stop her, she slid from the banquette, out on the floor and moved, head high, towards the foyer. Greg stood up, too, and then glanced swiftly about the crowded room and realized that to pursue her would only make them both that much more conspicuous. Grinding his teeth in a rage, he slid back into his seat and glared before him, more angry than he could ever remember being until this moment.

As Holly came up the two steps from the dining floor to the foyer, her eyes searched the crowd still waiting for a table and found Chuck who was moving toward her, looking puzzled and anxious.

"Will you take me home, Chuck?" she asked huskily. Chuck glanced back into the dining room where Greg sat and his jaw hardened.

"Surest thing you know, Holly," he told her, and spoke over his shoulder to his friends. "I'll be back by the time they find us a table."

Holly was too upset to catch the murmur of anger that swept over the group, led by the very pretty girl who was Chuck's date. Outside, in the moon-silvered night, beneath palms that rustled in the never still sea breeze, Chuck guided Holly to his car and put her into it.

As the car slid out of the parking area and into County Road, Holly put her head back against the back of the seat and two great tears slipped from beneath her closed lids.

"Oh, Chuck," she whispered, piteously, "I'm such a fool!"

"Aren't we all?" Chuck answered, glancing at her swiftly, seeing the path the tears made down her cheek. "Would it help any if I went back and beat the daylights out of Channing? Or is it just a lovers' quarrel?"

Holly shivered and shook her head.

"It's not a lovers' quarrel. We're finished. I never want to see him again — ever!"

"Seems to me that's a line I've heard a few thousand times before," Chuck mocked dryly.

"It's true, Chuck. And he'll never speak to me again!"

"Do you mind?"

"Mind? I don't want him to! I think I hate him. I'm almost sure I do!"

"That could be bad!"

Her interest caught, she turned her head and frowned.

"Bad?" she repeated, not quite sure she had heard him correctly.

"It always follows a lovers' quarrel," Chuck told her sagely. "They never want to see each other again; they never want to speak to each other again; they hate each other; and then — well, hate and love, so I'm told, are the two strongest human emotions, and it's incredible how close they are together, how easy it is to mistake one for the other."

"I'm not very wise about love, Chuck," she confessed humbly.

"Well, it's quite a subject. Requires an awful lot of study and close attention and considerable experience — or so I'm told," he answered cautiously.

"I thought he was in love with me, and that was why he was being so kind." Holly's voice broke as she tried to speak. "But he was just — creating a girl out of what I was when he first met me — like that man in the play. He wants to show me off now. He's like any artist who creates something and wants to show it off. He said that, Chuck. He admitted it."

"Well, blast his gizzard!" said Chuck grimly. "Show you off? Well, what else has he been doing all season? It's gotten to the point where no smart night spot or dinner place is considered officially open until you two are seen there — where else would he like to show you off? Or did he say?"

"At a dinner party your sister is giving."

Chuck's hands tightened on the wheel and the car slued to one side before he mastered it.

"He wants to take you to a dinner party at Caro's?" he asked. "What in blazes does he hope to prove by that, for Heaven's sake?"

"He wants to show your sister that the girl she ignored had potentialities, I suppose. Oh, I don't know! It's just that he seemed to feel it would be *fun* to march me into the villa, wearing a special frock of Cecelie's, and see if I could hold my own with your sister's guests, as if I was a piece of statuary, or a painting he'd created!"

Chuck swore under his breath and asked curiously, "And what did he think Caro would do — throw you out of the house when she recognized you? She wouldn't, you know. Caro's not like that at all."

"He wanted me to be insolent and arrogant."

"Oh, he did, did he?" Chuck obviously found that amusing, though it deepened his anger. "And just what had he planned to do to teach you to be so thoroughly unpleasant? Because you'd have to be taught, that's for sure. It's certainly not something that comes naturally to you."

"I knew I couldn't," she told him humbly. "I am very grateful to your sister and to her husband."

"Oh, Hubert's quite a guy," Chuck answered cautiously.

"Oh, yes," Holly agreed eagerly. "And Wilkins is nice, too. He was very kind — "

"But you saw very little of Caro, I take it."

"Well, she was busy, and after all, she didn't really *want* me there. It was your brother who insisted she have me."

"Thanks," said Chuck dryly.

She looked up at him, puzzled.

"For not saying I insisted that you stay with Caro," Chuck explained. "I didn't, you know. I just kept my mouth shut. And that was as bad. Silence giving assent, I suppose you'd call it."

"Well, I suppose all of you realized there just wasn't anything else you could do."

"Oh, yes, there was." Chuck interrupted. "We could have given you the money we got for the Hacienda, and you could have gone anywhere you liked and been independent."

Holly stared at him, wide-eyed.

"Oh, I wouldn't have known where to go," she protested.

Chuck looked down at her in the moonlight as the car slid to a halt besides the stairs to the apartment. She was very lovely, he told himself, even without the added enchantment of the moonlight.

"No, I suppose not," he agreed at last. "I suppose it was best that you stay with Caro. Anyway, you've done all right for yourself, haven't you?"

Her young face was crumpled momentarily by the threat of tears, but she managed to control herself as she got out of the car and walked to the foot of the stairs, Chuck beside her.

"Oh, yes," she stammered bitterly. "I've done all right for myself. I've made a colossal fool of myself — and now I don't know what's going to happen to me."

"Hi, now," Chuck protested, and yearned to take her in his arms and hold her close. "You stop that! What's going to happen to you? A lot of good things, wonderful things! I'll see to that.

She looked up at him, and the moonlight, splashing in a silvery-white flood about them beyond the reach of the tall palms and the dense shrubbery, showed him her astonished young face.

"Oh, you mustn't worry about me," she stammered.

"Why not?"

"Well, after all, the Lamonts have done quite enough for me," she said faintly. "I'm not a child, even if I have been behaving like one with Greg. I can take care of myself."

"Famous last words!" Chuck mocked her lightly. "Look, are you *quite* sure you've finished with Greg?"

"Oh, *yes!*" There was a touch of grimness in her voice that convinced him that she spoke the truth.

"Then how about having dinner with me tomorrow night so we can make some plans for your future?"

Even in the moonlight he could see faint color on her cheeks and stars in her eyes.

"I'd like that!" she answered simply, and added hastily, humbly, "if you're quite sure you want me."

Chuck studied her for a moment longer, and then he grinned.

"I was never so sure of anything in my life," he told her firmly. Before he turned to his car, his eyes swept over her in the exquisite frock, and his jaw hardened slightly. "But not in a Cecelie frock, Holly. Something of your own, shall we say?"

Holly looked down at the lovely frock, all silvery lace with great splashy pink satin roses appliqued against the lace. Her hand brushed it disdainfully, and she answered quickly, "I'm never going to wear anything again that doesn't belong to me!"

"That's the spirit." Chuck grinned. "I'll pick you up tomorrow at seven?"

"I'll be waiting," she assured him eagerly, and as he got into his car and drove away, he knew somehow that she would.

15

THE night was so beautiful that Holly sat down on the steps leading up to the apartment and drew a deep, hard breath. All around her she felt the warmth of the night, the faint breeze scented with orange-blossoms from a nearby estate, with the almost too heavy scent of a night-blooming jasmine distilling its fragrance beneath the dew's caress; and the moonlight on the old house and the gleam of the lake beyond made a soothing picture.

Her thoughts were jerked back to the present as a pair of headlights turned in through the old stone gate posts. She was pinned against the shadows behind her as a car crept smoothly up the drive and stopped.

She stood up, blinded by the lights, puzzled and frightened. Then she heard the car door slam shut, and a man walked across the beam of the light. Her heart gave a startled jerk — it was Greg who was coming toward her. As he passed out of reach of the lights and faced her, his back was to the moonlight and she could only guess at his expression. His tone when he spoke left no doubt that he was still in a cold, towering rage.

"You were in such a hurry to go off with young Lamont you forgot your wrap," he told her, and thrust it out to her, a wadded bundle of ivory satin lined with shocking pink that matched the flowers scattered over her lace frock.

"Oh, thank you — ," she stammered. She took the bundle and shook it out carefully, draping it about her shoulders.

"I want to talk to you," Greg told her shortly, and caught her wrist and pulled her toward the car.

"Oh, but, Greg, it's late. Couldn't we talk tomorrow?" she protested, even as they reached the car and he thrust her into it.

"We'll talk tonight," he told her shortly. "Tomorrow I shall be far away."

He slammed the car door on his side, and the powerful motor purred as he slid the car back down the drive and into the Trail.

"You're going away?" Holly asked faintly.

"Did you think I'd stay here and let you make me the laughingstock of the whole resort?"

"Oh, Greg, I'm so *terribly* sorry," she apologized.

"You're going to be a whole lot sorrier before I've finished with you," he assured her grimly as he turned into Royal Palm Way and across the bridge over the lake and swung into Flagler Drive, heading south.

"Greg, where are we going?" she asked uneasily as the car picked up speed.

"Miami."

Holly caught her breath and drew the inadequate folds of the ivory and pink stole about her bare shoulders.

"But, Greg, I can't go like this."

His eyes slued toward her for just a moment, and the light from a street lamp they were passing showed her his face, cold and set and contemptuous.

"Why not? It's one of Cecelie's best."

"But, Greg, at least let me pack a bag. I can't elope like this."

His savage bark of laughter was like a slap in the face.

"Elope?" The word, in that tone, was an insult.

Holly blinked beneath the ugly impact of his tone.

"Then what are we going to Miami for?" she managed at last.

"I'm leaving for Europe as soon as I can get plane passage," he told her grimly. "I'll drop you off down there. From then on, it'll be up to you. Oh, you'll make out all right. Your kind always does."

Anger crowded out the uneasiness

and the fear in Holly's mind and she cried spiritedly. "You, of all people, have no right to say that — 'my kind' — "

"No? Then what should I call you? A girl who takes greedily with both hands and a sweet air of innocence anything a man can give her, and then when he asks a simple thing of her, like attending a formal dinner party, who cuts and runs straight into the arms of another man?"

"It wasn't like that at all, Greg," she protested hotly. "I didn't want to go to Caro Beardsley's dinner party. I didn't want to be put on display like a painting or a piece of furniture. I do have some pride."

"Oh, do you now? That's interesting," Greg sneered, and the car gained speed, as though his cold fury had lent it extra momentum. "I *am* surprised. Not enough pride to prevent me from showering you with expensive clothes — "

"They were returned to Cecelie as

soon as I'd worn them."

"And you think Cecelie would put second-hand clothes back in stock?"

Holly blinked. "Then what did he do with them?"

"Sent me the bill, which I paid, and delivered the stuff to my apartment. What else did you think he'd do?"

"But he said he only wanted me to display them."

"Which you did, because I took you to the places where they were meant to be displayed." Greg wearied of the subject, and his eyes on her were bitter. "I think I'm furious with you on more than one count. It's not pleasant for a man who prides himself on being a good judge of women to be so completely taken in by a wide-eyed little doll like you! It will be very hard for me to forgive that."

The road stretched away from them, wide, straight, with hammock-land on one side, tall dunes on the other.

"Please, Greg," she burst out, "don't drive so fast!"

"Scared?" he sneered as though he enjoyed making her uncomfortable. "This car does a hundred and twenty miles an hour, see?"

As her wide eyes clung to the speedometer, she saw the needle creep up from 75 to 80 to 90. Holly cried out, her cry torn from her, flung into the wind they created with their own speed. The needle climbed another notch to 95, and Greg laughed. For the smallest instant his eyes were off the road, watching her, gloating over her terror, and in that instant it happened.

The car veered no more than a few feet, and yet it was enough to send it swinging to the side of the road, onto the soft shoulders. There was a wild screaming of brakes that would not hold and, it seemed to Holly, an age when the car seemed to waver, to teeter. Then it plunged over the embankment and down, with a great crashing of metal and glass. She had fumbled with the door in her frantic terror, and the impact sent the door open and Holly spinning out into the darkness of oblivion.

Stunned, unconscious she lay where she had fallen.

Later, how much later she could not know, there came to her very vaguely the sound of cars stopping, excited voices, the roar of flames, and a loud cry, "Hi, he wasn't alone in the car. Here's a girl."

Gentle hands lifted her; somebody cried out, "Don't touch her! Don't try to lift her. Wait for the ambulance and the doctor."

An ambulance screamed through the night and stopped while two white-coated men ran to the palmetto thicket where Holly lay. Swift, expert hands lifted her to a stretcher, and the ambulance screamed once more through the night while an excited crowd, to which two county police had been added, fought the flames that were roaring over what had once been Greg's cherished Mercedes.

Connie stirred, raised a sleepy head

and scowled at Jan.

"For Pete's sake, Jan — ," she protested.

"Connie, it's after three o'clock, and Holly isn't in," Jan sid anxiously.

Connie thumped her pillow resoundingly and snapped, "So what?"

"Connie, I'm worried."

"She's out with Greg Channing, and that guy always watches the sunrise before he goes to bed," Connie said grimly. "Get some sleep, Jan — the kid can take care of herself."

Jan wandered out into the living room, carefully closing the door, wondering how Connie could be so unconcerned.

She picked up the telephone book, and, turning her back on the clock, dialed Greg's number. There was a long delay in which she heard the telephone ringing clamorously. Then a man's voice, very wide-awake, said sharply, "Mr. Channing's residence. What is it, please?"

"Could I speak to Mr. Channing,

please, if he's there?" asked Jan.

"Mr. Channing, madam, died in a motor crash an hour ago," stated the man with a stark simplicity that struck Jan like a blow.

"Oh, no!" she gasped.

"The police are here, madam. The young lady has been taken to the Good Samaritan Hospital," said the man firmly, and put down the telephone with a decisive click.

Jan sat for a stunned moment, wide-eyed and dazed. Greg Channing was dead! And 'the young lady' was in the hospital! She had no doubt that the 'young lady' was Holly. With shaking hands she sought and found the hospital number and called it.

"Could you *please* tell me the identity of the young woman in the auto crash with Greg Channing?" she asked when a briskly impersonal voice had said, "Good Samaritan Hospital," in her ear.

"We haven't been able to identify her," answered the voice. "She is in emergency and we haven't been able to question her. If you think you know her, we'd be very glad if you would come over and identify her, if you can."

"I — yes, I'll be there as soon as I can," Jan answered, and put down the telephone with a shaking hand.

Connie roused again as she hurried into the room and began dressing.

"*Now* what?" demanded Connie.

"Greg Channing has been killed in a car crash. There was a girl with him. It could be Holly, Connie. I'm on my way to the hospital to identify her if I can." Jan flung the words at her as she dashed out of the room.

"Well, forevermore," sighed Connie, and ran her fingers through her tumbled hair, all thought of sleep completely gone.

16

INSIDE the hospital lobby, dimly lit, silent save for the telephones behind the reception desk and the faint whisper of rubber-shod feet on waxed and shining floors, Jan looked swiftly about her.

A young nurse behind the reception desk smiled a brisk, impersonal smile, and Jan explained her mission. The nurse's smile faded and curiosity touched her eyes as she directed Jan down the hall and to the Emergency Operating Room.

Outside the door Jan hesitated, and a young interne came swiftly out of the operating room, looking startled at sight of her. Jan once more explained why she was there.

"Oh, yes, the girl in that Channing smash," he agreed. "They've just finished operating and are about to take her up to the recovery room. But we're anxious for her to be identified. Just a minute, please."

He went back into the room and came out, holding the door open for her, smiling encouragement as Jan hesitated at the sight before her.

A middle-aged, very tired-looking doctor said briskly, "This way, please. Do you know her?"

Jan stood beside the wheeled cart and looked down at Holly. Holly who was a stranger, so white that her skin had a bluish tinge. An enormous bandage partially concealed her dark hair, an arm bandaged from wrist to shoulder, and beneath the thin covering sheet, the stiffness of the young body, its shapelessness indicated a cast of some kind.

"Well?" asked the doctor, very tired but not without compassion. "Do you know her?"

"I — yes, of course," stammered Jan, badly shaken. "Will she live?"

"It's too soon to tell," the doctor

answered. "Who is she?"

"Her name is Holly Tolliver."

"Are you a relative?"

"No, I don't think she has any relatives. I'm a friend — a close friend."

"I see," said the doctor, and motioned to the two attendants, who swiftly bore the cart out of the room, a nurse following.

"Here," said the doctor to Jan, and offered her a glass of pungent, aromatic spirits of ammonia. "It's quite a shock, seeing someone you are very fond of in her condition. But you may be quite sure that we'll do everything in our power for her. At least she's much better off than that poor devil, Channing. These speed demons — " He swore under his breath, and Jan drew a deep, hard breath and steadied herself with an effort.

"He was killed, his servant said," she managed.

"Nasty mess. His car caught fire, and I'm sure you can guess the rest," said the doctor. "You'd better run along now and get some rest. Your friend will be unconscious for some time. You can see her later. It may be much later before she can be questioned."

Something in his tone caught Jan's attention, and she repeated, "Questioned?"

The doctor seemed to be surprised.

"Well, naturally the police will want details about the accident, how it happened and why it happened. Since she is the only survivor, they will want to question her as soon as that's possible," he pointed out.

"Yes, of course — how stupid of me," Jan stammered, and made her escape.

She never quite remembered how she drove back to the apartment. When she reached it, Connie was in the living room in a robe and slippers, and one look at Jan's white face stopped her question.

"Here, drink this," Connie ordered, and put a cup of hot coffee before Jan.

"Oh, Connie, she looks so dead" wailed Jan, and covered her face with her hands.

Connie's eyes widened in shock. "*Is* she?"

"The doctor said it's too soon to know whether she's going to live or not," Jan said shakily. "But she looks — oh, Connie, I'm so afraid for her."

"Here, drink your coffee and pull yourself together," Connie ordered, her brows furrowed. "I wonder if we ought to notify the Beardsleys or the Lamonts? Do you think they'd be interested?"

"Oh, Connie, we should never have brought her here! We should have left her with them. Maybe then she'd have been safe."

"Well, it's a sure thing she'd never have met Greg Channing if she had stayed there," Connie admitted.

"It's all my fault, Connie." Jan's tears had broken her control.

"Oh, for Pete's sake," snapped Connie sharply. "Stop that foolishness. You tried to warn her about Greg

Channing, and what good did it do?"

"I know, Connie, but she's such a kid, too young and too innocent to know what was good for her."

"And too stubborn to take your advice!" Connie reminded her. "It's a shame, Jan, and I'm terribly sorry for her, but I won't have you blaming yourself!"

"Who else is there to blame?"

"That snooty Beardsley dame who tucked her off into the servants' quarters and forgot about her."

Jan shook her head.

"I assumed the responsibility for her."

"That you did, pal, that you did!" Connie agreed dryly. "Speaking of warning people — you may remember I told you at the time — "

"Oh, Connie, don't!" wailed Jan, and burst into a storm of weeping.

Connie, alarmed at such a breakdown, put her arms about Jan and said sternly, "Now you stop that! It's not going to do her a bit of good for you to go to pieces like this. You'll only hurt yourself. We'll wait until the morning at a respectable hour and then, if you want me to, I'll telephone Papa Beardsley."

Jan shook her head, smiling damply.

"No, that's my job!" she insisted. "And, Connie darling, you've got to work tomorrow. You should be getting some sleep."

"Some sleep, she says!" Connie poured another cup of coffee, lit another cigarette and rumpled her tousled hair. "I don't feel as if I'd ever sleep again!"

"But you must, Connie. Tomorrow is my day off, but you have to work," Jan urged her. "Come on; let's give it a try anyway."

But long after Connie had fallen asleep, Jan lay wide-eyed in the darkness, unable to get out of her mind the picture of Holly as she had seen her at the hospital, or to rid her thoughts of the conviction that she had meddled outrageously in bringing Holly from the villa.

It was very near dawn when at last she fell into an exhausted sleep from which she woke to find the room flooded with sunshine and a note propped up against her bedside clock. As she picked up the note, she saw the hands of the clock were pointing to twelve.

'I left the car for you, honey,' Connie had written. 'I knew you'd want to go to the hospital, and I can thumb a ride from the bridge. You might pick me up at the office at five, if you're free. And don't worry!'

Connie had underscored the last three words heavily, and Jan felt she could hear Connie's voice speaking those words — Connie, who pretended to be so hard-boiled and who was really butter-soft inside.

Jan showered, dressed, had a cup of coffee and a glass of orange juice and set out for the hospital. The doctor had told her Holly would be under sedation for at least twenty-four hours, but she had to be there in case Holly awoke. Somebody had to be there, and Holly had no one else.

She hesitated a moment at the thought of telephoning the Beardsleys. Then she recalled Holly's terror at the sight of Walker Lamont and her frantic insistence she would never go back there. Her mouth thinned a little. Undoubtedly the Beardsleys as well as the Lamonts had already lost interest in Holly, so why turn to them now?

She drove back across the bridge and up Flagler Drive to the hospital's parking area. Inside the lobby, she went straight to the reception desk, where several young nurses, very crisp and immaculate in their starched uniforms and their white caps, presided.

"Miss Tolliver?" one of them said, smiling her pleasant impersonal smile as she turned to the revolving card file beside her and skimmed it with swift competence. "Oh, I'm sorry. Her condition is critical. No visitors."

"There's been no change since last night?" asked Jan hopefully.

"I'm afraid not. That was the report that came down half an hour ago," answered the nurse, and turned to another anxious caller.

Jan turned blindly away from the reception desk and stumbled against a man who was just emerging from the admissions office. She offered dazed apologies without looking up, the man caught her arm and steadied her and she looked up into Hubert Beardsley's kind, concerned face.

"Why, it's Miss Wilkes, isn't it?" he greeted her.

"Why, yes, Mr. Beardsley," Jan replied. "I wasn't sure whether I should telephone you when I heard about Holly."

"Wilkins brought me the morning paper," Hubert answered and drew her with him to a quiet corner of the big reception room. "Have you any idea how it happened? They told me you came over early this morning to identify her. How did that happen?"

When Jan had finished she tried very hard to smile at him, but it was a ragged and quite unconvincing smile.

"I can imagine how you must be feeling about me," she stammered, "for dragging her away from the villa. This would never have happened if she'd stayed there — so you see, it's all my fault."

Hubert stared at her, obviously shocked.

"My dear girl!" he protested. "That's idiotic! She's been very happy, I'm sure — and how could this possibly be your fault?"

"I promised you I'd take care of her, and I'm afraid I've failed miserably," Jan answered huskily. "But I *did* try to warn her about Greg Channing. I felt he was much too old and much too sophisticated for a girl brought up as Holly had been. But she wouldn't listen — and now this *awful* thing — "

She looked up at him and her eyes were filled with tears.

"She may die. Has she any chance at all?"

Hubert said quietly, "The doctors aren't sure yet how much of a chance she will have. Everything possible that medical skill and science can do, will be done."

"I'm sure of that, of course," Jan told him huskily. "It's a very fine hospital — a great place for miracles and I'm afraid that's what it's going to take — isn't it?"

Hubert nodded reluctantly. "I'm afraid so, Miss Wilkes. But please stop blaming yourself."

"But if she'd stayed at the villa, she would never have met Greg."

"She would have been a very unhappy little girl, though," Hubert pointed out with a gentle smile. "As it is, you've given her something I am sure she must always have longed for, a warm and enduring friendship. She's had a lot of things all young girls dream of: pretty clothes, good times, a very attractive boy friend — though

I'm afraid Greg was scarcely a boy."

They were silent for a moment, and then, his brow furrowed with a puzzled frown, Hubert said slowly, "What I can't understand is what they were doing at that hour of the morning more than halfway to Miami."

"Oh," asked Jan, "is that where the accident occurred?"

"So the newspaper account said. A few miles below Ft. Lauderdale."

Jan considered the idea for a moment, and then she asked incredulously, "They couldn't possibly have been eloping?"

Hubert obviously thought that extremely unlikely.

"Why should they elope? Greg Channing has no one to answer to — nor had Holly. And if they were trying to avoid publicity, or the three-day waiting period, they would have been heading north to the Georgia-Carolina line, where I understand it's possible to be married in a matter of hours."

Jan nodded and her mouth drooped. "And somehow I can't imagine Greg Channing wanting to marry a girl as young and — as unsophisticated as Holly, can you?" she asked.

"I'd met Channing," Hubert admitted cautiously. "In fact, he was an invited guest at a dinner party my wife is planning. I believe he would have brought Holly as his dinner companion. But I can't quite picture him marrying anybody. He'd always fought shy of marriage."

"Well, we can't know anything until Holly is able to tell us, can we?" Jan said huskily, and stood up. "I don't suppose I'd be allowed to see her, would I?"

"I'm afraid not," Hubert said regretfully. "No visitors, not even relatives."

Jan's soft mouth twisted.

"Relatives!" she repeated bitterly. "That's one of the things that makes Holly so pathetic to me. She *has* no relatives, not even a distant cousin. It's just not right for any human being to be so alone!"

"She's not alone, Miss Wilkes, as long as she has a devoted friend like you," said Hubert quietly.

"I'm afraid I haven't been very good for her."

"That's nonsense, and I'm sure you know it quite as well as I do," he protested strongly, and with his hand beneath her elbow, guided her out of the hospital and across to her car. "I'd like to ask you to have lunch with me, but I don't imagine you are in the mood for that. Later, perhaps, I hope."

Jan looked up at the vast, many-windowed hospital, and her chin quivered.

"I hate to go away and leave her," she said, fought for her self-control and managed a small, twisted smile. "Which is pretty silly, since everything possible is being done for her, and there's nothing I can do but sit in the reception room and bite my nails. And that wouldn't be very helpful."

"No, I'm afraid not," Hubert agreed, making an effort to rise to her attempted relief of the tension. "You go and get some rest, and the moment there is any change, or she is able to talk, I'll call you. That's a promise."

"Thank you, Mr. Beardsley," said Jan, and added impulsively, "I can understad now why Holly was so very fond of you."

Hubert looked faintly surprised but very pleased.

"Oh, was she? I didn't know," he admitted.

"Why are we speaking of her in the past tense? Not she *was* fond of you, Mr. Beardsley — she *is*! I know it somehow! She couldn't change! It's not in Holly to change."

She managed a faint smile and slid beneath the wheel of the car. As Hubert stood back watching her, she slid the little car out of the parking area and back into the thickening traffic of Flagler Drive.

17

SHE did not notice the car parked just below the big old gray house as she turned in at the driveway and stopped beside the stairs to the garage apartment. But before she had gone more than halfway up the stairs, the car followed her into the drive and she turned, puzzled, as a tall, darkly good-looking young man in sports shirt and flannels got out and came toward her.

"You're probably Jan," he stated. "Holly thinks an awful lot of you. I'm Chuck Lamont."

Jan stiffened. Another of the Lamonts, eh? She wasn't feeling very kindly disposed toward the Lamonts, although Walker was all right, she supposed.

"Yes, Mr. Lamont?" she said coolly. "What can I do for you?"

Chuck stood at the foot of the steps,

looking up at her. He was hatless, and the wind stirred his thick dark hair slightly. His eyes were dark and hard as marbles.

"You can tell me what the blue blazes Holly was doing out riding with Greg Channing at that hour of the morning, as a beginning," Chuck stated flatly.

Jan's eyes flashed as she thrust out her chin belligerently.

"I'm afraid I can't see what business that is of yours, Mr. Lamont," she said icily.

Chuck took the steps two at a time until he stood just one step beneath her.

"Do we have to stand here on the steps? There's a heck of a lot I have to ask you, and you'd be perfectly safe to invite me inside. I'm house-broken." He flung the words at her out of his dark anger.

"Well, yes, come in if you like," Jan told him, puzzled.

Inside the pleasant living room she

turned to face him, her eyes cold.

"Well, Mr. Lamont?" she asked. "Why are you so interested — so late?"

And then she saw his twisted face and the torment in his eyes and was more puzzled than ever.

"I just don't get it." He ignored her question, his tone filled with anger and bewilderment. "She quarreled with Channing at the Hibiscus Club last night and walked out on him."

"What?"

"She asked me to bring her home, and of course I was tickled to death to do it," Chuck plowed miserably on. "She said she never wanted to see him again, that she hated him — oh, I know I shouldn't have taken her seriously when they'd just had a lovers' quarrel. But I *did* take her seriously; I asked her to have dinner with me tonight, and she seemed pleased at the idea. So *why* did she go tearing off with Channing a little later?"

Jan had listened to him in amazement.

When he turned to her, his dark eyes tormented by his question, she answered gently, "I don't know, Mr. Lamont. I can't imagine why."

"Unless she was just trying to make a fool of me, to get revenge on all of us for — for treating her so shabbily?" he suggested miserably.

Jan stared at him in bewilderment.

"I think you must have lost me somewhere, Mr. Lamont, I don't seem to understand," she admitted.

"Well, if she thought maybe she could get me to fall in love with her, and then she could laugh in my face — " He was obviously unwilling to accept that and yet unable to deny that it could be so.

"Oh, my goodness, Mr. Lamont — "

"My brother, Walker, is Mr. Lamont — I'm Chuck. You don't think that was what she was up to?"

"You don't know Holly very well, do you?"

"Well, no. I've seen her around with Channing and I've had a few dances with her, but last night was the first time I'd really been with her more than just for a dance," Chuck admitted, scowling. "So now I'm wondering if the whole thing — her quarrel with Channing, asking me to bring her home, being so sweet and gentle — if it wasn't all a part of a plot to get me to fall in love with her so she could laugh in my face."

"Believe me, Chuck, Holly's not that devious! Such a plot could never in the world have entered her mind!" Jan insisted firmly. "Why, I don't believe it could ever have occurred to her that there was the faintest possible chance you could even admire her, much less fall in love with her."

Chuck's eyes met hers steadily.

"It wouldn't be hard to do at all — fall in love with her, I mean," he said frankly. "She's beautiful and sweet and good and kind!"

"You know her better than you think you do, Chuck, for she is all of that."

"Then why in blazes was she out

with Channing?"

Jan sighed and spread her hands in small gesture of bewilderment.

"I'm afraid that's something only she can tell us, Chuck — when she's able to," she told him quietly.

"Do you think she will be — able to, I mean?"

"We'll have to hope, Chuck, and pray that she will. The rest is up to the doctors."

Chuck nodded and tore a cigarette to pieces as though he had no idea what it was doing in his fingers.

"Funny," he said at last, "I've known her for such a little while — and yet, somehow I have the queer feeling that I don't want to know any other girl — ever! That's funny, isn't it?"

Jan shook her head. "I don't think so. Holly's pretty special, and I've known her quite awhile."

Chuck turned toward the door and paused, his back to her. After a moment he asked, "You don't think there was anything wrong about her being out with Channing, do you?"

Jan felt the stiffening of anger through her body.

"Do you?" she asked bitingly.

Chuck turned to face her, and his jaw was set and hard.

"I don't know," he admitted. "But somehow, I feel that even if there was — it wasn't her fault. I know Channing pretty well — that is, I *knew* him. He was a devil with the ladies; he usually played around with a pretty worldly-wise crowd of gals. They all knew the score, and Holly must have been a pretty fascinating novelty to him. I think that's why he got so furious with her when she wouldn't agree to let him put her on display — as his own special creation."

Jan's eyes widened in angry surprise.

"That's what they quarreled about," he explained. "Greg had been invited to dinner at my sister's place and told he could bring his own dinner companion — which I don't understand, because Caro is always so fussy about her dinner parties, always two and two like the animals going into the ark. And I can't imagine her not pairing Greg off neatly with somebody in her own crowd, but apparently she didn't. And Greg was going to bring Holly, and show what he had done with her. He had 'created' her out of nothing."

Jan gasped in outrage and bit back the angry epithet she would have addressed toward Greg, had she not remembered in time that one must not speak ill of the dead.

Chuck nodded in understanding.

"That makes two of us," he seemed to read her thoughts. "So that's why they quarreled and she ran out of the Club. And of course she had to have a way to get home, so she asked me to bring her, and I jumped at the chance. My own date will probably never speak to me again, which at the moment seems to me of less than no importance at all."

Jan was still digesting the account of the quarrel, and suddenly Chuck burst out, "Then why the devil was she out riding with him a few hours later? Surely she wouldn't make up with him after he had humiliated her like that."

"No, I'm sure she wouldn't," Jan agreed slowly. "They have had a few light spats — not really quarrels. One was because she danced with you somewhere, I seem to recall. But he called her and patched the whole thing up. But this would take a lot more patching than that!"

"You said it." Chuck nodded grimly. "She cried all the way home."

"Oh, poor Holly!" Jan was stricken at the thought.

"So why would she go riding with him later?" Chuck was still worrying the thought like a dog with a bone.

"That's something only she can tell us, Chuck, when she's able to — "

"When!" Chuck repeated, and added anxiously, "You think it's when, Jan, not *if*?"

He looked so young, so anxious, so

deeply troubled, that Jan felt a little warm rush of tenderness for him, as though he had been a five-year-old begging reassurance.

"We have to hope, Chuck," Jan told him gently. "Everything possible is being done for her. She's young, healthy; I feel she'll make it, Chuck!"

"Do you? Honestly?"

"I do, Chuck, with all my heart."

Chuck drew a deep hard breath and managed a taut grin.

"Thanks," he said briefly, and turned and plunged down the stairs. Jan heard the sound of his car as it drove off and wondered uneasily if she had encouraged him with a false hope that might boomerang.

Holly was crawling slowly, painfully, torturously through a long long tunnel. Dense blackness pressed in upon her; she knew she had to keep crawling, to keep fighting because far, far away at the very end of that tunnel there was the faintest possible glimmer of light.

When, an age later, she had managed

to pull herself from the mouth of the tunnel, she lay too exhausted to open her eyes. Faintly there was a murmuring, so soft, so far away that she could not distinguish words though she knew the murmuring was human voices.

" . . . never walk again," one of the voices said.

"Does she know?" asked the other.

"Oh, no, of course not. And I hope not to be the one to have to tell her family . . . "

The voices faded into silence and Holly lay, eyes closed, exhausted by the struggle to regain some small measure of consciousness. When at last she could pry her heavy eyelids up, she saw the faint light that had guided her through that seemingly endless tunnel: a small, shaded light on a table beside her bed.

Dazedly, without turning her head, she let her eyes move and know that she was in a high, narrow hospital bed, and that darkness pressed close against the windows. She tried to move and realized that she couldn't. Her body was encased in something thick and heavy that restricted any movement save that of a heavily bandaged hand. And it hurt too much when she tried to move that.

She lay very still and let the tide of memory sweep over her.

"Greg!" she whispered, and then her eyes closed again as she seemed to hear the echoing crash of the car — the smashing of glass — the roaring of flames. She screamed beneath the impact of that memory, but the sound was no more than a very small whispered cry.

18

WALKER Lamont was waiting for Jan when she reached the lobby of the airport after completing her flight to New York. Somehow she wasn't surprised that he was waiting, but she was pleased.

"Holly's off the critical list, Wally," she told him joyously. "Isn't that wonderful?"

"Chuck called me this morning to tell me about it," Walker answered, smiling at her as he guided her out to his parked car and tucked her into it. "Funny, he's all broken up because she won't see him. I didn't know he was that deeply interested in her."

"I'm afraid you'll have to brace yourself, Wally," she warned him. "He wants to marry her, if he can. Would you mind very much?"

Walker stared at her in the brief

interval while waiting for a traffic light to change.

"Mind? Why should *I* mind? If it's what Chuck wants, then more power to him," he said firmly. "I barely know Holly; I've only met her a couple of times. But from what you tell me about her, I'm sure Chuck would be half-drowned in luck if she'd marry him. She will, won't she?"

"I don't quite know," admitted Jan. "And it has me worried. She's in an odd frame of mind — though I suppose after coming as close to being killed as she did, it's only natural that she'd be frightened and depressed."

"You don't think maybe she's grieving about Channing?" asked Walker.

"Oh, I'm sure she isn't," Jan answered eagerly. "She told me how that happened. He practically dragged her into the car against her will — she didn't go with him willingly. She hated him, I'm sure."

"And she can't have seen the papers, so she doesn't know that there are some rather scandalous implications about the accident."

"That's why I asked you if you would mind Chuck marrying her. To people who don't know her, she might seem a rather abandoned young creature."

Walker laughed at her. "Holly? Abandoned? Even as little as I know her, nothing could convince me that Holly could, of her own free will and accord, do anything scandalous or improper!"

"I'm so glad you feel that way! I so hoped you would. Because it's true! She's been foolish, I suppose, and she *has* gotten herself talked about — but she's really sweet and good!"

"If that's the way you feel about her, then that's good enough for me," Walker told her firmly. "She's a very lucky girl to have a friend like you to stand up for her so valiantly."

"Well, isn't that what friends are for — to stand up for you when you get yourself in a jam?" asked Jan lightly.

"Such friends are few and far

between, believe me!" Walker assured her, and added, "You're a pretty wonderful person, Jan. These last few days when I've waited for you at the end of your flight and we've had dinner together, while you gave me the news on Holly — I don't suppose you have any idea what that has meant to me?"

Puzzled, Jan eyed him curiously.

"I never dreamed you were that interested in Holly," she admitted.

"Don't be coy with me," Walker advised her with such unexpected vigor that she drew a little away from him and her eyes widened. "You know darned well what I meant. Of course I'm interested in Holly — but I could have gotten the news about Holly on the telephone without driving over here to the airport to meet you. This is the second such trip — and it has by no means been altogether to get news about Holly."

Once more a traffic light stopped them, and he looked down at her, a peculiar gleam in his eyes, his hands loosely relaxed on the steering wheel. That fire in his eyes widened her own and brought color to her cheeks. After a moment, as the light changed and he sent the car ahead, she drew a long, hard breath and her hands clenched tightly in her lap.

"Well?" demanded Walker when she showed no inclination to speak. "Aren't you going to ask me what I mean?"

"If you want to tell me, I'm sure you will," she replied, and told herself furiously that not even Holly could have sounded more inane or more youthful.

"I didn't think you'd have the courage to ask a question like that," Walker said with frank satisfaction. "We'll postpone the discussion until we get to your apartment and I'm not driving through this blankety-blank traffic."

"Just as you say," responded Jan, and tried not to sound too relieved.

He glanced down at her, and a grin

tugged at the corners of his mouth before he gave himself up to the task of driving. When at last they reached her apartment, he followed her into the living room and looked about him.

"Nice," he commented.

"Do you like it? I share it with three other stewardesses — our schedules are such that never more than two of us are here at once. Usually, since I have the shortest run, I'm here alone. Like tonight."

Her voice was low, breathless, a trifle hurried, and Walker stood looking down at her, warmth in his eyes, a grin tugging at the corners of his mouth.

"You like your job, don't you?" he asked, and it was so different from what she had expected him to ask that she blinked.

"Well, yes, of course."

"And you'd have to give it up if you got married?"

"Oh, yes — " She looked hurriedly away from him and added, her voice rising a little, "But I have no intention of getting married."

"Haven't you?"

"Well, no — of course not — "

"That's too bad. Because I have."

"Oh, are you getting married? Congratulations," she said brightly, and hoped with all her heart that her voice didn't reflect the sharp, hard jolt the news had given her. "Soon, I suppose?"

"That, of course, is for you to say," Walker told her pleasantly, "though I must admit I don't hold with long engagements."

Jan could not keep back the sharp, angry words, "Will you stop fooling and tell me exactly what you're talking about? You lost me somewhere."

"I'm talking about the fact that I'm in love with you and want to marry you. Hadn't you guessed?"

Jan made a little airy gesture and turned away from him.

"But that's utterly ridiculous." She spoke over her shoulder, and marveled inwardly that her voice could sound so light and airy.

"Ridiculous that I should want to marry you?"

"And ridiculous that you should imagine yourself in love with me." She was still being very airy about it, though she dared not turn to face him. "Why, you barely know me. We've met — what is it, half a dozen times? And we really shouldn't count that first time, when we fought so."

"Quite the contrary," Walker assured her pleasantly, and now there was a twinkle in his eyes and his voice echoed it. "That was when it happened. I'd never known before that a girl could be so furious and still be perfectly beautiful."

She turned then and stared at him, in wide-eyed and quite honest surprise.

"Beautiful? Me? Why, I'm not even pretty!" she protested.

"If I may quote — 'Beauty is in the eye of the beholder,'" Walker told her, and now there was no longer any hint of raillery or teasing in his voice. "To me, you are radiantly beautiful, because

I love you. It's as simple as that!"

Their eyes met and tangled and clung. There was a glory in hers, he saw with a leap of his heart, but there was uneasiness, too. He waited for her to find words to express whatever it was that was troubling her.

"But, Walker, it's too soon! We can't possibly know whether we're really in love — not when we barely know each other," she stammered at last.

Walker put his two hands on her shoulders and drew her close. He did not take her into his arms or kiss her. He merely held her so that they were very close. There was no laughter, no twinkle in his eyes, and his voice was deep, vibrant with tenderness.

"I don't want to stampede you, darling," he told her. "I know it has happened very fast. And I'll give you all the time that you need to get accustomed to the idea. All I ask is that you think about it, that you remember that I love you, and maybe one of these days you'll find that you — well, that you can like me a little — no, I take that back. I don't want you to like me; I want you to love me. Will you keep that thought in mind?"

Jan studied him for a moment. Then with a little smile that went straight to his startled, delighted heart, she put up her two hands, framed his face between them and, standing on tiptoe, set her mouth on his.

For the breathless, exquisite moment while the kiss endured, they stood so. His arms went about her, holding her very close, and his cheek against hers.

"That did it!" he told her huskily. "Up until a minute ago, I could have waited very patiently for you to make up your mind. But now — "

"Who's got to make up whose mind?" she mocked him, her voice tremulous with warm laughter. "I made up my mind about you a long time ago; I was just afraid you hadn't, about me. I wasn't sure you'd had time enough to get to know me."

"That's a project to which we

can devote the next fifty years or so, don't you think!" asked Walker, husky-voiced.

"Oh, fifty years, at the very least!" Jan told him happily.

This, she told herself as she gave herself to his embrace, was what Connie had been telling her about; Connie, who was so ecstatically happy in her engagement to her beloved Phil.

19

HOLLY lay so quietly when Jan came into the room that at first Jan thought she was asleep and would have slipped back out again. But Holly had heard her and turned her bandaged head. Her thin young face was touched with a faint smile.

"Oh, hello," she said wearily.

Jan studied her anxiously even as she returned the greeting and looked about the room massed with flowers.

"I was going to bring you some flowers," Jan told her. "But I can see it would only have been bringing coals to Newcastle. I've never seen so many outside a flower shop. Dare I ask who sent them?"

"It was Chuck," Holly answered, and her mouth thinned and twisted. "I wish he wouldn't."

"You're not being very kind to him, Holly. He wants very much to see you."

"I don't want to see him ever again."

"But, Holly, why? For heaven's sake, honey, he's not to blame for anything that has happened. He understands why you were with Greg when the accident happened. He doesn't hold it against you that you were out with Greg that night." Jan, puzzled, tried to reach the girl, to get an answer to the mystery.

Holly looked up at her, and Jan had never seen such misery in anyone's eyes.

"They haven't told you yet, have they?" Holly asked bitterly.

Frowning in bewilderment Jan answered, "Nobody's told me anything except that you are getting along splendidly and that you should be up and out of here in a matter of weeks."

"To spend the rest of my life in a wheel-chair?"

Holly's eyes clung to Jan's and saw the stunned, incredulous shock in them. Holly's smile was bitter and twisted.

"Oh, yes," she told Jan, who was too stunned to speak. "*I'm never going to walk again.*"

"Holly, that's not true!" Jan gasped. "Who told you?"

"Nobody told me. They're waiting until I'm strong enough to stand the shock," Holly answered harshly.

"Oh, then it's just a crazy idea you've got."

"No. It's true," Holly's voice cut across Jan's attempted reassurance. "The night I regained consciousness I heard voices, very faint and far away. And one of them said, 'She will never walk again.' It was two of the nurses, and they didn't know I was conscious." She turned her head on the pillow, and tears slid from beneath her closed eyelids.

Jan sat for a stunned moment, trying to accept the terrible news.

"But, Holly, that can't be true!" she

said at last. For all her effort, she could not quite get the conviction in her voice that she felt should be there. "The doctors would have told me — or Mr. Beardsley — "

"The other nurse said, 'I'm glad it isn't going to be my job to tell the family'," Holly said huskily. "Don't you see, Jan? That's why I'm in this cast. My back is injured. Oh, it's true, Jan; it's true."

"And that's why you have refused to see Chuck?" Jan probed gently.

"It's why I haven't wanted to see anyone except you and Hubert. He's always been so kind, and I'm so grateful to him." Holly's voice broke, then mended itself after a moment. "I don't want to see Chuck ever again."

Jan stood up, her eyes flashing.

"Well, I just don't believe that you're going to be — that you won't walk again," she said swiftly. "I'm going to have a talk with the doctor. You wait right here — " She broke off, flushing at the phrase.

Holly's smile was sadder than tears. "Oh, I'll wait Jan. I'm not going anywhere," she drawled, and Jan flushed and hurried out of the room.

Holly lay with her face turned toward the window. The sky was so blue, so shiny. There had been a shower in the night and the sky seemed to have been scrubbed and freshly shined by the rain. The breeze stirred the curtains ever so gently, and the scent of the flowers massed about the room spread their delicate perfume.

There were tears on her cheeks when the door opened to admit Jan and Dr. Jordan, the stout, middle-aged, tired-eyed doctor who had looked after her since she first came to the hospital.

Now Dr. Jordan looked angry, and Holly's eyes widened as he stood at the foot of the bed and looked at her as though he didn't like her very much.

"Now what's all this nonsense your friend has been telling me?" he demanded curtly. "That you're crippled? That you'll never walk again?"

"I heard the nurse, Doctor — " Holly stammered.

"And you feel so important that you consider yourself the only patient in the hospital? You just took it for granted there was no one else here, so they *had* to be talking about you?" snapped Dr. Jordan.

To Holly the room seemed suddenly flooded with a light far more golden than the sunlight, and she could only lie there against her pillow, her wide eyes probing his, searching, hoping for assurance yet afraid of accepting it.

"They didn't mean *me?*" she whispered at last.

"They didn't mean you." Dr. Jordan was tired and cross and saw no reason he should conceal the fact. He had worked very hard over this patient and had prided himself on doing a most excellent job. "My dear young lady, didn't it ever occur to you to ask a simple question, instead of holding this wrong thought and brooding over it, and making our job much harder?

A patient owes a duty to a doctor and to the nurses — the genuine effort to co-operate, to fight to get well. And here you have been making no effort at all. There have been times when I've wondered if you were grieving about that Channing fellow."

"Oh, I haven't, I haven't!" Color had crept into Holly's too thin young face, and her eyes were wide. "I just thought if I was going to be crippled I'd rather not get well."

"Well, thanks for that!" snapped Dr. Jordan irritably. "I'm sure all the people here who have worked so devotedly and so conscientiously to help you will be happy to know you were just dragging against us. I swear, I can't understand you young people. All of life ahead of you, and you moan and mope and fight against living it."

"Then I don't have a back injury?" asked Holly, too obsessed with her own thoughts and emotions to be entirely aware of his anger, or to resent it.

"Well, certainly you've got a back injury, and a bad one. Why the blazes do you think you're in a cast?" snapped Dr. Jordan. "Furthermore, you should spend a great many hours on your knees thanking the good God that you escaped with no more than that. You could easily have been slashed to ribbons, being flung out of a racing car and landing in a palmetto thicket. I still don't understand how you escaped with only some very deep gashes that, fortunately, did not become infected. And that, too, is something for which you should thank God every day of your life. You lost a lot of blood; that's probably why the gashes didn't become infected."

"But I've tried to move my legs and I can't!" she wailed.

"I should hope not! The cast was partly to prevent that, partly so that the pulled vertebrae could mend properly," he snapped. "But never walk again? For two cents, I'd take a paddle to you. I may do it, too, as soon as we get that cast off and get you up on your feet again."

"I'm sorry, Doctor," she pleaded.

"And so you should be! As a patient, I was very proud of what we'd been able to do for you, but to think you'd lie here holding such a thought and brooding about it and making our work that much harder — women!"

"I *am* sorry," Holly repeated.

"Then prove it by getting yourself up and on your feet again, young lady," Dr. Jordan snapped. "After all, there are other people who need that bed, and you would have been out of it much sooner if you'd had the grace to ask a simple question and get this crazy idea out of what passes for your mind."

He gave her an angry look and turned and strode out of the room.

Holly lay staring wide-eyed into space. And Jan waited, trembling slightly from the relief of knowing that Holly had been wrong, that the few words she had heard had not applied to herself.

"So that's why you wouldn't see Chuck," she said at last when it was apparent that Holly was beyond speech.

"Jan, I'm not crippled!" Holly whispered. "Oh, Jan."

"Well, of course you're not, you silly!" Jan bent and kissed her cheek. "Now get busy and get yourself well. Dr. Jordan was so angry when I asked him — when I told him what you thought — it wouldn't surprise me a bit if he *threw* you out!"

"He won't have to, now," Holly said radiantly. "I'll walk out of here one of these days — and we'll have a picnic on the beach — you and Connie and I!"

"And Wilkins will bring us a very luxurious basket of all kinds of fancy food and drink!" Jan laughed. "Let's make it very soon, Holly."

"Oh, we will," Holly promised eagerly, and added shyly, "Is Chuck still in town?"

"He's much closer than that," Jan assured her. "He's downstairs in the reception room, driving the nurses out of their minds because he keeps on insisting on seeing you and refusing to believe it when they tell him you don't want to see him. He seems to feel they are plotting against him, that you con't possibly be that cruel."

"He's awfully nice, Jan, isn't he?" Holly asked huskily.

"Nearly as nice as his brother Walker," Jan answered.

"Oh, do you know Walker?" Holly shrank a little.

"Know him? I'm going to marry him one of these days!" Jan boasted.

Holly laughed. "Oh, does he know it?" she asked.

"Why, yes. Matter of fact, it was his idea!"

"Jan! I thought you were just kidding!"

"Believe me, honey. I kid you not. See?" Jan held up her hand so that the sunlight winked on the diamond that graced the significant finger.

"Why, Jan, I'm stunned. I didn't

know you knew him that well!" Holly gasped.

Jan smiled tenderly at the diamond, twinkling with a thousand fires in the brilliant sunlight.

"I didn't, either," she confessed. "But it seems I do. Of course *I'd* known for quite a spell — but I was surprised when he got the idea, too!"

She stood up briskly.

"And now I'm going down and put Chuck out of his misery," she announced blithely, "and send him up for five minutes, which will be as much as the nurses will allow, I imagine."

She looked down at Holly and said, her tone one of gay mockery, "*You* a cripple? Holly, how silly can you get?"

Holly laughed as Jan went out and the door closed behind her.

Left alone, Holly reached for the bellcord at the head of her bed and pressed it hard. A moment later the door opened to admit the nurse, who looked startled as she saw the change in Holly.

"I'm going to have company," Holly announced. "Please help me. Do I have anything to put on over this hospital gown? And maybe some makeup?"

"Well, do tell," the nurse mocked her as she hurried to help her. "This is the day I've been looking forward to for many a blue moon; the day when you decided to wake up and live!"

20

CHUCK stood just inside the closed door looking at Holly. His young face was taut and his eyes were cautious.

"Hello," he said tentatively.

"Hello," said Holly, and politely, "Thank you for all the lovely flowers."

Chuck brushed that aside impatiently.

"Jan just told me why you've been refusing to see me, and I think you ought to be ashamed of yourself," he accused her hotly.

"I am," Holly admitted, and looked it.

"Even if what you heard the nurse say had been true, that didn't give you any right to refuse even to speak to me. What am I, a monster? I could have helped you feel sorry for yourself — because that's what you were doing, of course," Chuck plowed on grimly.

"And that's a pretty rotten thing, too — feeling sorry for yourself. Even if it was true — why, Holly, there are other people a whole lot worse off."

"If you came in here just to quarrel with me — " Holly began.

"I didn't, Holly," Chuck interrupted her. "It's only that it makes me so darned mad! I've been hanging around this place until I wouldn't have been surprised to have them lock me up in the observation ward to check my sanity. I've given up my job — "

"Oh, Chuck, no!"

"It was either that or get fired. I've been away from Canaveral so much lately, and I haven't been much good at my job what little time I've been there."

"Oh, but, Chuck, that's a terribly important job."

Puzzled, he asked, "What is?"

"Well, launching missiles and trying to hit the moon."

His eyes were wide with astonishment. "*Who's* launching missiles and shooting at the moon?" he demanded.

"Well, if you're at Cape Canaveral, aren't *you*?"

Chuck laughed. "I'm a sort of glorified office boy on a real estate subdivision as near there as we can get," he informed her firmly. "It's a Lamont project, and because my name is Lamont they had to find something for me to do; something that doesn't require much brains, of course."

"Oh, Chuck, I know that's not true!" Holly protested warmly. "Why, you have lots of brains."

"Some I've never even used?" he suggested, his eyes touched with laughter.

"Well, maybe. But you're awfully smart — I know you are."

The laughter vanished and he leaned toward her.

"You don't know anything at all about me, Holly."

"Well, that's as much as you know about me, which is a little less than nothing at all," she reminded him, flushing beneath the look in his eyes.

"I know," Chuck nodded soberly. "We don't know each other at all, but I think we should do something about that, don't you? I have a hunch you and I could be very good friends if we gave ourselves a chance."

Holly's eyes met his and could not turn away, and the color deepened in her face.

"Oh, I hope so, Chuck," she whispered softly.

Chuck leaned closer, and his eyes were warm, caressing.

"It's up to you, Holly." His voice was low, deeply serious. "If you'll let me sort of hang around — give us a chance to get acquainted — who knows what may happen? It could be sort of fun to find out, don't you think?"

"Oh, yes," Holly breathed, her eyes shining. "Lots of fun!"

"That's what I think," Chuck told her, and stood for a moment, looking down at her curiously. "You know, Holly, it's a funny thing. I've imagined myself in love a lot of times. But somehow it was never quite this way that I imagined it."

"Wasn't it? How did you imagine it would be?" she asked, as though fearful of what his answer would be.

"Oh, I don't quite know," he confessed slowly, and it was obvious that he was turning his thoughts this way and that, turning them inside out so they could both understand something that he was finding very difficult to express. "I suppose I imagined moonlight and roses and an orchestra playing softly somewhere in the background."

"And the loveliest girl in the world in your arms," Holly whispered huskily.

"Well, no, it wasn't quite like that! Oh, I supposed she would be beautiful. That's the kind of girls I like," he admitted quite honestly. "But I thought she'd have a lot of spirit and fire and be able to hold her own anywhere."

Holly's mouth had drooped, and there was the shine of tears in her eyes.

"So you see how fantastic it would be for you to imagine yourself in love with me," she pointed out, and added hastily, "Oh, not that I ever expected you'd be, of course."

"Why not, Holly? You're lovely."

"And full of spirit and fire and able to hold my own anywhere?" Her smile was thin and mirthless, for all its valiant effort to be gay.

Chuck was scowling as he studied her.

"Do you know something?" he mused aloud. "I began to realize a good while ago that the girls with so much fire and spirit were usually wrangling and fighting and insisting on having their own way. I believe a girl more gentle and self-effacing would make a mighty fine wife. Make a man feel her need for his protection and his backing — make him feel ten feet tall and very important to know she was leaning on him."

Holly held her breath, afraid to speak for fear of interrupting his train of thought which he was pursuing relentlessly, almost as though he had forgotten that he was speaking aloud.

"I feel very sorry for Hubert," he said at last. Holly blinked, unable to follow his thought, but waited for him to explain. "He's really quite a guy; only Caro rules him with an iron hand, and I can't feel that would be much fun for a husband. She never asks him about anything; she tells him what to do, what she expects, what she intends to do. If she ever asked his advice or his help, the poor dope would fall flat on his face in astonishment."

"He's *not* a dope," Holly flung at him with such unexpected spirit that Chuck's eyebrows climbed a little above his surprised eyes. "He's a darling! He's wise and kind and gentle — and so is Wilkins. They were both so good to me. And I won't have you calling him a dope! Do you hear?"

"Yessum," said Chuck meekly, and there was a twinkle far back in his eyes. "And I wonder where I ever got the idea that you are lacking in spirit."

"Well, I can fight for something or somebody I'm fond of, and I'm very fond of Mr. Beardsley," Holly told him swiftly. "I'd be an awfully ungrateful so-and-so if I wasn't fond of him after all he did for me. Why, I was outside of everything that was fun! Mary, the maid, was kind, and Wilkins was kind, too. But Mr. Beardsley — well, he took time and patience to make me feel like a human being, not just a bit of furniture that can be tucked into storage and forgotten! So you're *not* to call him a dope!"

"Yessum," Chuck repeated meekly. "You're quite a girl, Holly — yes ma'am, quite a girl!"

"Because I don't want you to make fun of Mr. Beardsley?"

"Well, that and other things as well," Chuck admitted cautiously. "Anyway, we're going to have a lot of fun getting acquainted. And who knows what may happen after that?"

The nurse came in, smiling her

pleasant, impersonal smile, and said briskly, "I'm sorry; visiting hours are over. Our patient must rest now, Mr. Lamont."

"Oh — sure," said Chuck, and stood up, smiling down at Holly. "I'll be back in the morning," he began

"Chuck, don't come back in the morning."

Alarm touched Chuck's eyes.

"Hi, now, wait a minute," he protested.

"I mean it, Chuck," she pleaded. "Go back to Canaveral and your job and come down weekends. I don't want you to throw away your job just on my account."

"But, Holly, I've already resigned."

"If it's a Lamont project, they'll take you back — they'll have to," Holly insisted. "And, Chuck, having a job — doing some work you like even when you don't need the money — is terribly important. Playboys are — well, they aren't much fun to know."

Her color was high and her voice

faltered, but her eyes met his, and there was a plea in them that somehow touched Chuck to the quick.

"Then I'll see you during the weekend," he said gently and saw the delight in her eyes.

"Oh, Chuck, I'm so glad," she breathed softly.

Suddenly aware of the nurse still waiting in the doorway, Chuck straightened, grinned at her and walked out.

The nurse stood for a moment watching Holly's illumined face, and then she, too, turned and walked out.

Holly was scarcely conscious of her departure. She lay very still, the deepest joy of her life flooding her whole being. It had been the most wonderful day!

She sighed blissfully, and when the nurse came with her supper tray she beamed happily and said, "Oh, whatever it is, it smells wonderful! And I'm starved!"

"Well, hooray for love!" the nurse teased as she settled the tray for her.

"I've always heard love is about the greatest stimulant known to science. Personally, I've never had the chance to try it."

Holly said, flushed and starry-eyed, "Oh, it's not love! I mean — Chuck's not in love with me — yet! And maybe he won't ever be."

"Oh, come now," protested the nurse, laughing. "You've seen him for five minutes; the hospital staff, from the orderlies right on up to the Chief of Staff, had had him in their hair for the last two weeks or more. If that guy isn't in love, then he should turn in his membership and start studying to be a misogynist."

Holly stared at her, wide-eyed, for a moment forgetting her hunger.

"What's a misog — what you said?" she demanded.

The nurse laughed. "You're not likely ever to meet one, my dear — and surely not in that young man who just left. A misogynist is a man who hates women. And a misogamist is a man who hates marriage."

"Oh," said Holly very softly, "like Greg."

"Undoubtedly," the nurse agreed, and added, "I don't think you need to worry; your young man is neither! You can safely take my word for it."

Holly studied her for a moment.

"You're terribly smart, to know all those words and what they mean." She was quite humble about it.

The nurse's pleasant, plain face with its bony structure, the reddish hair streaked with gray beneath the saucy little cap that went so ill with that plain face, was touched with a twisted smile.

"When you're neither young nor beautiful, and men aren't interested in you, and you've never known much about love, you have lots of time to acquire a lot of other knowledge," she said firmly. "But take it from me, Holly, knowing about love is far the more important. Just you remember that!"

"Oh, yes," Holly told her softly. "I will!"

"Good night," said the nurse, and went swiftly out of the room as though ashamed of her revelation . . .

Hubert looked up from his book and rose as Caro came into the library, sleekly groomed as always, stunning in her shining black dinner dress. The long soft white gloves added an effective contrast and her pearls shimmered in muted acknowledgement of the white of the gloves.

"How charming you look, my dear," said Hubert politely, trying not to reveal his surprise at her visit or at the quite unaccustomed touch of uneasiness in her eyes as they avoided meeting his.

"Hubert, may I talk to you?" she all but stammered, and Hubert was bewildered.

"Of course, my dear. What's wrong?" he asked quickly.

She selected a cigarette from the

hammered silver box on the table, bent her head gracefully to accept the light he offered and then looked up at him, crushing out the cigarette as though she had forgotten why she had picked it up.

"I had a talk with Chuck this afternoon," she said. "I should say he had a talk with me — at me, really, for he didn't give me much chance to talk back."

"Well, I suppose he was in a hurry to get back to his job."

"Hubert, have I been a good wife to you?"

Startled, bewildered, Hubert said, "Why, what an absurd question."

"Have I mistreated you, used you shabbily, ignored your wishes?"

"Caro, what on earth are you talking about?"

"About what Chuck said this afternoon."

"Well, you should have told him to mind his own business."

"He says I never consider you when

making plans, that I never ask your advice, that I dominate you." Her voice broke. After a moment she went on before he could speak, "I've never meant to be or to do any of those things, Hubert — take advantage of you. I love you very much, Hubert — more now than when we were first married."

"Why, Caro, my dear, you're crying — and you never cry."

"Chuck made me ashamed," Caro admitted huskily.

Hubert took her into his arms, and Caro clung to him, her face hidden against his shoulder.

"Do you know, Hubert, how long it's been since you held me like this?" she asked after a long moment, as her own arms tightened about him.

"Oh, not so long, I'm sure." He tried to smile comfortingly at her.

"I'm ashamed to remember how long it has been, Hubert," she confessed with a humility so at variance with her usual self-assurance that Hubert knew

Chuck must have used some pretty plain language and reminded himself to have it out with Chuck when he saw him again.

"Was it because I've neglected you, Hubert? Ignored you?"

"Oh, for Heaven's sake, Caro, you're being absolutely ridiculous."

"It wasn't because you'd stopped loving me?"

Hubert looked down at her so blankly that she had to accept that as a denial, even before he spoke.

"I'd never stop loving you, Caro my dear!" Hubert told her swiftly. "You're so busy — and have so many things demanding your attention."

"Nothing is ever going to demand my attention so much that I neglect you, Hubert!"

"Chuck must be out of his mind."

"I don't think so," Caro said frankly. "He seems to be very much interested in Holly; you know he used to say she had no spirit and he couldn't stand a spiritless girl. But today he reminded me that I had been a rotten wife to you."

"Why, the young — "

"And pointed out that I never considered you or consulted you."

"That's only because you know that whatever you want, whatever it takes to make you happy, is what I want too, so what is there to discuss or consult about?"

"You're sweet, Hubert!" She was smiling, misty-eyed.

"So are you, darling, and very lovely." Hubert kissed her as he had not kissed her in a long time and felt the warmth of that kiss tingling through his veins. Abashed by the emotion, he reached for a trace of raillery. "There! I've smeared your lipstick! You'll be late for the Hildreth's dinner."

"I'm not going," she decided suddenly, and flung her gloves and her small jeweled evening bag on a chair. She looked up at him, flushed and younger-looking than he had seen her in longer than he could remember. "Hubert, let's do something young and silly and romantic!"

Hubert laughed at her. "Such as what, for instance?"

"Oh, let's go out on the town, just the two of us! Dinner somewhere gay and giddy, a movie, dancing — and let's take a wheel-chair ride along the Trail and watch the moon come up over the ocean."

"Oh, come now," Hubert protested.

"Please, Hubert!" she begged, and then looked reluctantly at his books and up at him. "Unless, of course, you'd rather stay here and read a book."

"Nonsense! Let's go and be giddy!" Hubert agreed, and laughed at her. "I'm very flattered that you'd pass up the Hildreth dinner just to go out with me."

"Do you know why I don't go out with you more often, Hubert?"

"Because of your social activities, of course."

"Because you never ask me," she cut in simply.

"Oh, now, darling, you know I'm always anxious to do anything you ask."

Caro nodded, and the droop of her mouth was wistful.

"But don't you see, Hubert? I don't want you always to do what I want; I want you to express your own desires, make your own plans — and include me in those plans, please, Hubert?" Her voice was deeply earnest. "I do this very badly, Hubert — humble myself and ask for your love."

"It's been yours, darling, from the first."

"And until the last, Hubert? Funny, I've always felt self-sufficient and sure that my way was the right way. I didn't mean to get domineering and bossy. I'm ashamed of the way I treated Holly." She broke off and grimaced. "I'm glad we aren't having a tape recording of all this, because by tomorrow I'll probably hate myself. But right now — after the tongue-lashing I got from Chuck — "

"I'll give that young man a tongue-lashing of his own next time I see him."

"No, Hubert. He was right, and I'm grateful. It woke me up — made me see things more clearly. But of course I'm not sure it will last. You may have to take up where he left off, if I get out of hand again."

"I'll beat you twice a day, if you like," Hubert promised handsomely.

"Chuck thinks I richly deserve something like that." Caro smiled. "Do you think he's really serious about Holly?"

"I'm afraid he is. Would you mind very much?"

"Well, I don't suppose it would make the slightest difference to him, or to Holly either, if I did mind," she admitted with a faint trace of her old manner. "I admit I'd rather Holly hadn't gotten herself talked about with Greg Channing — but I dare say people won't hold it against her, and I'm sure there was nothing really wrong — aren't you?"

"Quite sure," Hubert assured her firmly, and added, "I have a strong feeling Walker is about to make an interesting announcement about his plans with Janet Wilkes."

"Janet Wilkes? Do I know her?" Caro frowned.

"She's Holly's apartment-mate, the airline stewardess. She and Walker have been seeing quite a lot of each other. I notice she's wearing a very handsome ring on the appropriate finger — and she blushed when I asked if she'd seen him lately."

Caro thought about her two brothers for a moment, and then she sighed, smiled and made a little gesture of dismissal.

"Well, after all, Walker is quite old enough to know his own mind, and I'm sure he wouldn't welcome any attempted interference from me," she said. "And the same is true of Chuck.

I admit I'd rather they had chosen girls from their own social circles, but after all, the really important thing is that they get married and keep the name from dying out."

"Yes, I suppose that *is* important," Hubert agreed dryly.

Caro looked up at him swiftly.

"The Lamonts have been in Florida for generations, Hubert. You don't think I want the name to die out?" she asked anxiously. "Our babies aren't Lamonts, remember!"

"That they aren't," Hubert agreed firmly, and then put his arm about her. After all, how much could he expect her to change? She had already softened so amazingly that his heart was beating faster at the realization of his long-buried but never dead love for her.

"If we're going out on the town, hadn't we better get started?" he suggested, and held out his hand to her. "I'll have Wilkins bring the car around."

"And you drive, and let's have the top down. It's a glorious night," she said as she put her hand in his.

THE END

WITH SOMEBODY ELSE
Theresa Charles

Rosamond sets off for Cornwall with Hugo to meet his family, blissfully unaware of the shocks in store for her.

A SUMMER FOR STRANGERS
Claire Hamilton

Because she had lost her job, her flat and she had no money, Tabitha agreed to pose as Adam's future wife although she believed the scheme to be deceitful and cruel.

VILLA OF SINGING WATER
Angela Petron

The disquieting incidents that occurred at the Vatican and the Colosseum did not trouble Jan at first, but then they became increasingly unpleasant and alarming.

DOCTOR NAPIER'S NURSE
Pauline Ash

When cousins Midge and Derry are entered as probationer nurses on the same day but at different hospitals they agree to exchange identities.

A GIRL LIKE JULIE
Louise Ellis

Caroline absolutely adored Hugh Barrington, but then Julie Crane came into their lives. Julie was the kind of girl who attracts men without even trying.

COUNTRY DOCTOR
Paula Lindsay

When Evan Richmond bought a practice in a remote country village he did not realise that a casual encounter would lead to the loss of his heart.

ENCORE
Helga Moray

Craig and Janet realise that their true happiness lies with each other, but it is only under traumatic circumstances that they can be reunited.

NICOLETTE
Ivy Preston

When Grant Alston came back into her life, Nicolette was faced with a dilemma. Should she follow the path of duty or the path of love?

THE GOLDEN PUMA
Margaret Way

Catherine's time was spent looking after her father's Queensland farm. But what life was there without David, who wasn't interested in her?

HOSPITAL BY THE LAKE
Anne Durham

Nurse Marguerite Ingleby was always ready to become personally involved with her patients, to the despair of Brian Field, the Senior Surgical Registrar, who loved her.

VALLEY OF CONFLICT
David Farrell

Isolated in a hostel in the French Alps, Ann Russell sees her fiancé being seduced by a young girl. Then comes the avalanche that imperils their lives.

NURSE'S CHOICE
Peggy Gaddis

A proposal of marriage from the incredibly handsome and wealthy Reagan was enough to upset any girl — and Brooke Martin was no exception.

A DANGEROUS MAN
Anne Goring

Photographer Polly Burton was on safari in Mombasa when she met enigmatic Leon Hammond. But unpredictability was the name of the game where Leon was concerned.

PRECIOUS INHERITANCE
Joan Moules

Karen's new life working for an authoress took her from Sussex to a foreign airstrip and a kidnapping; to a real life adventure as gripping as any in the books she typed.

VISION OF LOVE
Grace Richmond

When Kathy takes over the rundown country kennels she finds Alec Stinton, a local vet, very helpful. But their friendship arouses bitter jealousy and a tragedy seems inevitable.

CRUSADING NURSE
Jane Converse

It was handsome Dr. Corbett who opened Nurse Susan Leighton's eyes and who set her off on a lonely crusade against some powerful enemies and a shattering struggle against the man she loved.

WILD ENCHANTMENT
Christina Green

Rowan's agreeable new boss had a dream of creating a famous perfume using her precious Silverstar, but Rowan's plans were very different.

DESERT ROMANCE
Irene Ord

Sally agrees to take her sister Pam's place as La Chartreuse the dancer, but she finds out there is more to it than dyeing her hair red and looking like her sister.